GAME FOR FIVE

Marco Malvaldi

GAME FOR FIVE

*Translated from the Italian
by Howard Curtis*

Europa
editions

Europa Editions
214 West 29th Street
New York, N.Y. 10001
www.europaeditions.com
info@europaeditions.com

Copyright © 2007 by Sellerio Editore, Palermo
First Publication 2014 by Europa Editions

Translation by Howard Curtis
Original title: *La briscola in cinque*
Translation copyright © 2014 by Europa Editions

Library of Congress Cataloging in Publication Data is available
ISBN 978-1-60945-184-4

Malvaldi, Marco
Game for Five

Book design and cover illustration by Emanuele Ragnisco
www.mekkanografici.com

Prepress by Grafica Punto Print – Rome

Printed in the USA

To my grandfather, and my grandmother

Caminante, son tus huellas
el camino, y nada más;
caminante, no hay camino,
se hace camino al andar.

Walker, your tracks
are the path, nothing more;
walker, there is no path,
the path is made by walking.

—Antonio Machado

CONTENTS

GAME FOR FIVE

Whsen you start swaying on your legs, when you light another cigarette to kill five more minutes even though your throat is stinging and your mouth is so furred up you feel like you've eaten a tarpaulin, and then the others also light cigarettes and linger a while longer—when all that happens, then it really is time to go home to bed.

It was ten after four in the morning, in the middle of August, and three young men were standing next to a green Nissan Micra. They had all drunk more than was strictly necessary, the owner of the Micra more than the others, and the others were now trying to persuade him not to drive.

"I'll take you home," said the shortest of the three, whose head was shaven everywhere except on the top of the cranium, which made him look like a palm tree. "Leave the car here and I'll take you home."

The second young man was trying to refuse. He had just come out of the disco, and in addition to having the blood-alcohol level of an unemployed Russian, his head was full of little lights that made it hard for him to think. All the same he was putting up a good argument.

"Fuck it, if my dad sees I left the car and came with you, he'll say 'You've come home drunk,' and he'll kick my ass. He isn't stupid, my dad."

"If your dad sees you come home in that condition," Palm-Tree Head insisted, "he'll kick *your* ass because you came home on your own, and *mine* because I didn't come with you, that's firstly. Secondly—"

"No, no, I'm going by myself. Don't worry, I'll get there."

"Why don't you say anything?" Palm-Tree Head anxiously asked the third point of the triangle, who had gone to the hairdresser that evening and requested—with a certain firmness, presumably—and actually been given the chance to leave with his polenta-blond hair charmingly decorated with purple streaks like a punk leopard. Two bright, cow-like eyes and a half-open mouth complemented his appearance in an appropriate fashion.

"If that's what he wants, it's up to him," was his verdict.

"That's dumb. What if he goes thirty feet and smashes straight into a tree?"

"Listen, I'm off. If I don't feel up to it, I'll give you a ring on my cell phone and you can come and get me."

Palm-Tree Head looked at his friend as if thinking, "Dammit, he's stubborn," and received by way of reply an even more vacuous look that meant: "I don't give a fuck, I'm going home to bed in a couple of minutes."

"Go on, then, we'll wait here for ten minutes. If—"

"Don't worry, if I'm not up to it I'll call you."

The young man had tried to speak clearly and without cursing, as best he could, to give the impression that it was passing. In reality, his head was still ringing, and if he moved it he had the impression the world was following him with a second's delay.

He took a deep breath, groped in his pocket for the key, and found it immediately, which seemed a good omen. He looked at it for a moment, approved its appearance with an unsteady nod of the head, and got in the car. He closed the door, turned the key, and set off—all things considered—without any problems.

After about half a mile, coming level with the parking lot by the pine wood, he had to stop. While he was driving, the car had seemed like rubber, swaying frightfully in one direction, without ever going in the other. It was like being inside a washing machine, with the drum turning around him. Swish, swosh, swish.

He opened the door, not without difficulty this time, and stepped out.

"I'm sure a bit of fresh air will do me good."

He was still making an effort to speak without cursing—even though he was alone—in order to convince himself that everything was fine. And also to keep awake, which wasn't easy.

"But now I have to urinate. Yes, I really do. Oh, yes. I think it's necessary."

As he was performing this soliloquy, he approached one of the trash cans.

It had rained the night before and the ground in the parking lot was still muddy, in spite of the heat. Avoiding the puddles, he reached the trash can and, with a brief mental speech, selected it as his personal urinal.

About a century later, as he was pulling up his zipper, he noticed there was a girl in the trash can. It also struck him that she was quite pretty. Almost simultaneously, something told him that she was probably also dead. He wasn't immediately surprised. Rather, preserving a calm that only alcohol could have given him, he started to think aloud. Contrary to what we read in mystery stories, the discovery had not helped to clear his head.

"Do I know her? No, I don't think so. I have to tell the police. I'll go to the car and get my cell phone."

He did so, and discovered that the battery of his cell phone was completely flat.

"Fuck, that's all I need. What do I do now?"

He looked around as if there was someone there who might suggest an answer.

"Wait, wait. I saw a bar on my way here that was open. Now, take a deep breath. I have to concentrate and stop seeing everything turning, or I'll never get there."

Before getting back in his car, he opened his hands and concentrated on them for two or three minutes. Paradoxically, he felt relieved: he had been afraid to go home at this hour in the state he was in, and the discovery of the body would justify both the delay and his blood-alcohol level, given that someone who finds a dead body is entitled to something strong, isn't he? *Ergo*, at least he had gotten past the fear.

"There, now everything's fine. Keep calm, just follow the white line and you'll get there."

He did in fact get there, after another minute of fear, and walked straight to the door of the bar. Pull yourself together, he told himself mentally, then turned the handle of the glass door and went in. Behind the counter, the barman was washing and putting away glasses. He gave him a curious look. The young man tried to appear cheerful, which merely emphasized the state he was in, and asked with a smile, "Excuse me, do you have a phone?"

"Behind the ice cream freezer."

He was about to go and phone when an inner voice stopped him. He raised one finger and asked, "Do I have to order something?"

"The phone works just fine without it," the barman said.

He reached the telephone, dialed the number, and said, "Hello, is that 113? Listen, I have to tell you that I found the dead body of a girl in a trash can, she's really dead, I'm sure of it."

A brief silence.

"Yes, in the parking lot by the pine wood, where the Germans go for picnics, but I think the girl is Italian, she has dark hair."

A brief silence.

"Yes, in a trash can. The gray one near the parking lot for camper vans, the one where the Germans go. Yes, for picnics."

A brief silence.

"Yes, I know I'm drunk, you don't have to tell me that, but this is true! Really . . . Sorry to say this, but you're as stubborn as a mule! It's true . . . "

Silence.

He stopped and looked at the phone for a moment.

"They hung up," he said, incredulous and vaguely offended.

Meanwhile, the barman had come out from behind the counter and was looking at him with a mixture of surprise and severity. "Is there really a body?"

"Damned right there is. It's in the parking lot by the pine wood, the one where—"

"Yes, I got that. Come on, we'll go there together and you can show me, then *I'll* call the police."

The barman took his cigarettes from the counter, lit one, glanced at his watch, and walked outside, followed by the young man.

"Give me the keys, I'll drive."

BEGINNING

The only pleasant thing to do, at exactly two in the afternoon on a day in mid-August, when the air you're breathing is liquid and you're trying not to think that it's still six or seven hours to dinner time, is go to a bar and have a drink with a few friends.

You sit down at one of the tables outside, adjust your pants—the crotch of which is so wet it needs wringing—cool off for ten seconds, and magically become yourself again. Whoever in your group is feeling in good form goes inside to order from the counter, because when the barman saw you he glared at you and is now washing glasses (or rather, one glass—the same one for the past five minutes) and if nobody goes inside to order, forget it.

The important thing, though, is that there's a bit of a breeze.

That wisp of wind, just strong enough to lift your shirt away from your skin a little, gently count your vertebrae, and cool the gaps between your toes—to which your plastic flip-flops have given very little relief thus far—but not so strong as to ruffle the hair you've brushed over your bald spot. The iodine smell of the sea breeze unblocks your nostrils and persuades you to breathe, and by the time the hero who has taken on the job of a waiter returns with the drinks and the cards, you're feeling in a good mood again and the afternoon has suddenly gotten a hell of a lot shorter.

Such things are pleasant at the age of twenty. At eighty they are the salt of life.

The little group outside the Bar Lume, bang in the middle of Pineta, consists of four sprightly old-timers of a type common in these parts. The two other once common types, old men with walking sticks and grandchildren and old women knitting in doorways, cannot compete numerically and are thus seen with decreasing frequency.

On the much reviled threshold of the twenty-first century, Pineta became, to all intents and purposes, a fashionable seaside resort, and so the associations promoting the locality have been inexorably extinguishing the above-mentioned categories, turning the very architecture of the town against them. Where there was once a bar you could play bowls at there is now an open-air disco-pub, an open-air gym has materialized in the pine wood to replace the playground where you used to take your grandchildren, and it's impossible to find a bench, only stands for motorcycles.

The four men must be quite good friends, to judge by the way they are arguing: three of them sitting with Papal dignity on plastic chairs, one standing with a tray bearing a pack of cards, a Fernet Branca, a beer, and a Sambuca with a couple of coffee beans. One of those sitting is writhing on his chair as if bitten by a tarantula.

Clearly, something is missing.

***

"What about my coffee?"

"He didn't make one."

"He didn't make one? Why?"

"He says it's too hot."

"What do I care if it's too hot or not to drink coffee? As if it isn't bad enough my daughter counting the cigarettes I smoke, now the barman starts worrying about my health? Let me deal with him!"

Ampelio Viviani, 82 years old, retired railroader, decent former amateur cyclist and uncontested winner of the cursing competition held (unofficially) as part of the *Unità* festival at Navacchio from 1956 for twenty-six consecutive years, gets proudly to his feet with the help of his stick and heads boldly for the bar.

"Look at him go, he looks like Ronaldo!"

"It must be the way he holds his stick!"

Reaching the counter, he aims his stick straight at the barman. "Massimo, make me a coffee."

Massimo has his head bent over the sink. He is slicing lemons, and seems totally absorbed in the operation, like a Buddhist monk meditating. In the same ascetic fashion he replies, "No coffee. Too hot now. Later. Maybe."

"Horseshit! Listen to me, I fought in Abyssinia and you think it's too hot here for me to drink coffee?"

Still with his head bowed, Massimo retorts, "It isn't too hot to drink it. It's too hot to make it. You really want me to stand here in this Turkish bath, sweating like an ox? All for a lousy coffee that wouldn't even come out right, with all this humidity? Have an iced tea, on the house."

"Iced tea! If I'd wanted to feel sick I'd have stayed at home with your grandmother and watched the TV news! This is the last time I set foot in this bar."

At last, Massimo raises his head. He's about thirty, with curly hair and a beard. There's something vaguely Arab about his appearance, accentuated by his loose, knee-length pirate-style shirt miraculously devoid of patches of sweat. He has a sulky, sidelong way of looking at people. He raises his eyes to heaven for a moment, briefly, untheatrically. Then, with his eyes once again on the lemons, he says, "Look, Grandpa, this is the only bar in the whole of Pineta where anyone can stand you, and that's only because it's mine. So if you want a coffee, just wait a few hours, you don't have a job to go to."

"Give me a grappa, and to hell with my daughter!"

By the time Ampelio gets back to the table, Aldo, the owner of the Boccaccio restaurant, is shuffling the cards.

"*Scopa*, *briscola*, or *tressette*?" he asks.

The other two regulars sitting at the table raise their heads. The first to open his mouth is retired postal worker Gino Rimediotti, who looks all of his seventy-five years, and who now says, as he usually does, "I'm fine with anything. As long as I don't play in a pair with him there."

"Listen to him! As if it's always my fault . . . "

"Yes, it is your fault! You never remember what cards have been dealt even if they bite you."

"Gino, listen, I'm fond of you, but someone who winks like he's swallowed gravel the way you do should just keep still, OK? When you're dealt a three anyone would think you're having a heart attack. Even the people inside the bar know what cards you have."

The name of the fourth man is Pilade Del Tacca. He has watched seventy-four springs glide pleasantly by and is happily overweight. Years of hard work at the town hall in Pineta, where if you don't have breakfast four times in a morning you're nobody, has formed both his physique and his character: apart from being ill-mannered, he's also a pain in the butt.

Aldo stops shuffling. The crucial moment has arrived. In a neutral voice, he says it's ridiculous that it's always he or Ampelio who has to choose, and then Del Tacca always complains. "Either you choose, or we do something else."

"I don't mind choosing," Ampelio says, "but if you don't like it we can change the pairs."

"If who doesn't like it?" Del Tacca asks.

"Your whore of a mother!" Gino says. "Who do you think? All of us."

The air has turned heavy, you can't feel the breeze anymore.

In the silence, Massimo comes out of the bar, grabs a chair, and joins the little group.

He lights a cigarette, and takes the cards. "I left the girl to mind the bar," he says. "There's nobody about at this hour. How about a game of *briscola* for five?"

There isn't even any need to exchange glances. There's a gleam in their eyes now. They empty their glasses, put their elbows on the table, and away they go.

A game of *briscola* for five is always welcome.

Some six months earlier, Ampelio's voice had rung out as usual over every other noise in the bar, skillfully illuminating the twists and turns of his mind—he was someone who never missed the opportunity to communicate *urbi et orbi* his opinions on every subject under the sun.

"What I don't get is what people see in it! They shut you up in a big room with the music blaring out, you're all crowded together one on top of the other, you can't dance, all you can do is wriggle about like you had sand in your underpants, and by the time you leave your mind's all befuddled. And they actually make you pay to be treated like that! Now you tell me if that's normal . . . "

"Grandpa, first of all, lower your voice and stop making such a fuss. Thank you. Now, what do you care if people want to enjoy themselves that way? Are they hurting anyone?"

Ampelio put down his glass. "I tell you who they're hurting!" he went on. "Themselves, that's who! I say if they want their ears to ring, they should bang their heads a few times with a hammer, at least it's free . . . "

Aldo stood up to get his lighter from the pocket of his coat.

It was the day the Boccaccio was closed, and being a carefree, gregarious widower, he liked coming to the bar in the evening because he was sure to always find someone there.

"The problem is," he said as he tried to get the lighter out without his overcoat falling off the rack, "so many kids these days only enjoy themselves if what they do costs a lot. Not that there's anything new about that, let's be clear. It's just another way to look cool, to show that you have money. Except that fashions change. Right now, luckily for me, it's fashionable to pretend to know about wine. If only you saw how many kids come in after dinner, take the wine list and then call you over. 'What I'd like is a . . . ' and maybe they confuse the name of the producer with the name of the wine, or else they want an '87 Chianti, which if they knew the least thing about it they'd know that an '87 Chianti is no good for anything but lighter fuel, and then as if that wasn't enough they eat cheese with honey. The hardest part is to agree with them without laughing."

"You should just tell them they don't understand a damned thing," Pilade cut in with his usual politeness, "and then set them straight on a few matters. That way they'll learn little by little."

"Oh, yes, they'll learn little by little, and then they'll go somewhere else," Aldo replied. "They don't want to drink well and eat well, they just want to show off how cool they are for knowing about wine. Let them do what they like. I sell food and wine, I don't give lectures."

One thing has to be recognized: whenever Aldo asserted that he sold food and wine without frills he was absolutely right. The Boccaccio offered an extensive cellar, with a particular leaning toward Piedmont, and exceptional cooking. Period. The service was good, if informal, and the décor was not especially elegant. Moreover, if anybody ever happened to express any disappointment with the food, this would somehow always reach the ears of the chef, Otello Brondi, known as Tavolone, who, although endowed with incomparable talent in the ancient culinary arts, had not been greatly blessed by the Muses in any other respect, and so the critic would often find him looming over the table, with his thirty-five cubic feet of belly and two thick forearms as hairy as a bear's, asking, "What do you mean, you don't like it?" in a not exactly accommodating tone.

Aldo lit his cigarette. "Personally," he went on, "I hate places where if you order a wine not perfectly suited to what you've chosen to eat, or if you try to bend the rules of Gastronomy with a capital g, they treat you as if you're some kind of hick and say, 'No, no, no, why do you want to spoil that saddle of rabbit off the bone with a green bean and cashew nut flan? If only you'd listen to me . . . ' or even worse. I know places where there's no middle way, either you're a connoisseur and then the owner loves you and always gives you a star entrance, or you're a piece of shit who doesn't know a damned thing about wines and then they make it pretty clear to you that someone like you should stay at home and not come around there breaking balls, because there are people waiting. They don't mind your money, they just can't stand you."

This speech was greeted with complete silence.

Wednesday was never a very busy day, plus there was a biting wind outside, which every now and again blew the lids off the trash cans and rubbed the branches together and howled under the double-glazed door. Only the noise gave any idea of how cold it must be out there.

Massimo had had enough of standing behind the counter pretending to be a barman, so he came out through the flap and made a timid attempt to get rid of the old-timers—they were nice guys, but they did get on your nerves after a while—so that he could close up and go home.

"It must be more fun anyway, going to the disco than playing cards. Didn't you have a game tonight?" he said, craftily putting the night in the past tense, hoping in this way to make it clear that he was about to close.

"Hey, you're right, we still have time," Ampelio said.

"But there are five of us," Massimo said, cursing himself inwardly. "You're always forgetting I stay open after midnight so you can play cards, but I don't think games for five people have been invented yet."

"You may have a degree, Massimo, but you really are ignorant. Haven't you ever played a game of *briscola* for five?"

"No."

"You've never played a game of *briscola* for five? Ampelio, what did you teach your grandson when he was little?"

"To ask his grandmother three times for chocolate and give half of it to him when they had him on rations because of his diabetes."

"What an idiot, your grandpa. Listen, how about giving it a go? I'm sure you'll like it. I've never known anyone who doesn't enjoy *briscola* for five."

Massimo thought it over. It was bitterly cold outside and the idea of going out there wasn't especially inviting.

That'll teach me to be clever, he thought. But the idea of avoiding the cold for a while longer wasn't a bad one.

He went to get his cigarettes. Outside, the wind was making the shutters whistle, and the street lamps were swaying, lighting the street only in flashes that made it look truly ghostly. He made himself a coffee without asking the others if they wanted any, went to the table, sat down, and stretched his legs. Then he put his elbows on the arms of the chair, lit a cigarette, and said, "Go ahead."

The four old-timers took their chairs and made themselves comfortable at the table without the usual round of cursing. In fact, their whole attitude had changed to a mixture of satisfaction and concentration, as if they were the repositories of a great secret and were pleased to have found someone who could appreciate it.

Pants were straightened, sleeves rolled up, and cigarettes placed religiously on the table, as if to underline to themselves that they were really going to need them. The typical behavior of those savoring something in advance.

Even Massimo's mood had changed. As he watched the old-timers getting ready he had started to feel something. It was like when you're a little kid and the older children ask you to play with them, of their own accord, without their mothers forcing them to do so. You're being allowed to take part in a ritual, whatever dumb thing you get up to you have a lot of fun, and you end up with a day to remember. For a fraction of a second, he wondered if thinking that playing cards with four old geezers was a lot of fun mightn't be a symptom of something strange about him, but he immediately dismissed the thought.

Can I at least decide what I like? he thought, and focused his attention on the High Priest who was about to open the gates of the Temple to him.

"So," said Pilade, who was acting as master of ceremonies, "this is how it works: the cards are dealt, all at the same time, eight cards per player. Then you do the auction. Each person in turn declares how many points he thinks he can win on the basis of the cards he's holding. For example, the auction starts at sixty, the first person says 'I win with sixty-one,' the second says, 'I win with sixty-three,' and so on, until one player fixes a value so high that the others give up. Whoever wins has the right to choose the *briscola*, like this: let's say you have an ace and a three of a particular suit, do you follow me?"

"Yes, yes, I follow you."

"Then you should call the king of that suit. You say 'king of whatever' and that way you establish two things. One, that the *briscola* is that suit. Two, that your partner for that hand is whoever has the king of that suit. The other three are against.

To win you both have to score the points you declared at the beginning. It's good to win the auction because that way you get to choose the *briscola*, but you have to play to win while the others play to make you lose. Plus, you're two against three."

"But once the teams have been formed, how do you know when it's your turn?"

"You just go around the table. The nice thing about the game is that *you don't know who's playing with you.* As soon as you've said the card, all four of you start giving each other dirty looks, and accusing each other of being the intruder, and saying they don't have any cards of that particular suit. One of them is lying. But until that card turns up you have no idea how the game is going, neither you nor your opponents. Only the player who has the king knows the whole situation, and obviously he'll do everything he can not to be found out, he may even lose lots of points to hold off being discovered as long as possible. Did you get all that?"

"Deal the cards, and let's give it a go."

He had gotten home at four in the morning, after dumping Grandpa Ampelio on the couch, because Grandma Tilde went to bed at eleven and bolted the door of the bedroom and whoever was out stayed out.

He had really enjoyed himself. And ever since that night, whenever the customers allowed it, he'd played *briscola* for five and had a whole lot of fun.

TWO

About an hour and a half had passed and the game was over. Pilade had won, Massimo and Aldo had put up a good fight, and Ampelio and Rimediotti had been a disaster. As Massimo, once again forced to be a barman, gathered the glasses, the four old youngsters laboriously shifted their chairs in the direction of the sidewalk. Having transformed the vicious circle into a parliamentary amphitheater, they were now ready for what, in Pineta, was the national sport.

Sticking your nose in other people's business.

"So, did you see? There's even been a murder now."

"I know. Just imagine! A poor girl murdered in her own home! It's already dangerous enough on the streets with all these Albanians around, now they kill you in your own home."

"Gino, I'm sorry but, firstly, can you tell me what the Albanians have to do with it, and secondly, how do you know she was killed in her own home?"

"She was wearing slippers, fur slippers. Nobody walks about outside in fur slippers apart from crazy old Siria. That means she was killed in her own home."

"Poor thing . . . "

Massimo, who was emptying the overflowing ashtray in the bucket, couldn't stop himself from asking, "But where do the Albanians fit in?"

Gino looked up at him, gave an upward jerk of his chin (an

age-old gesture, intended to reinforce one's own opinions almost as if invoking divine knowledge for oneself: it is indispensable in barroom arguments, especially when dealing with subjects about which there might be a number of different viewpoints, such as the performance of a center-forward, a woman's familiarity with oral-genital practices, and so on) and said, "Why, don't you agree? Do you think it's right for all these people to come here, without papers so you don't even know who they are, and I'm supposed to believe they're all decent people? They're all crooks! They deal drugs, they steal, they think they're God knows who . . . "

"What I meant," Massimo continued wickedly, "was where do they fit in this time? Can you explain to me why every time something happens you bring up the Albanians, even when that woman had her bag snatched outside the Lomi baths?"

Gino flushed and for a moment lost the thread of what he was saying. Three weeks earlier, a woman bather had been robbed of her bag outside that particular bathing establishment, and the old man had held forth for two days about the Albanian peril, prophesying every kind of misfortune and demanding that the government take action. It had gone on until the evening of the third day, when it emerged that the thief was the grandson of one of his neighbors.

***

Taking advantage of the moment, Pilade now joined in the debate. "How do you know about the slippers?"

"Massimo was telling us before you got here," Gino said somewhat stiffly. "He was the one who found the poor girl."

"So now you've dropped the Albanians and you suspect me?"

"You found her, did you?"

"Not exactly, a guy who was near the trash can found her.

When he found her he tried to call the police, but his cell phone was flat. As this bar was the only place open at 5:15 he came here to call the police, only he was dead drunk, so the switchboard operator thought it was a joke and hung up. I went with him to see where the body was, and then I called the police. They arrived five minutes later, they identified the girl within ten minutes, and since they'd already called the doctor they all looked a bit . . . "

Massimo broke off for a moment, passed the cloth over the table, and shook it over the bucket. He didn't have to make an effort to remember that morning: he recalled everything very distinctly.

He liked Dr. Carli, all things considered, and when he arrived at the parking lot by the pine wood Massimo was curious to see how he would react to seeing someone he knew in the trash can. He did know her, even if only by sight, because she was the daughter of a good friend of his.

The doctor had lived up to his reputation of being a seraphic person: he had immediately recognized the girl, and had only stood there for a moment, looking at the body, before shaking his head dubiously.

He hadn't seemed upset: he may already have suspected something when he arrived. Nobody had had the presence of mind to look him in the eyes after he got out of the car and greeted the police officers. Only after examining the body, with a delicacy that was unusual in him, had he let himself go a little.

"You know what the problem is?"

Massimo said nothing, continuing to look the doctor in the eyes—eyes that now betrayed a touch of anxiety. It was clear that he had no desire to go home: most likely, he preferred the role of the efficient doctor to that of the grief-stricken friend.

"The problem is that I have to tell Arianna."

Precisely, Massimo thought.

"And you don't want to?" he asked. It was a stupid question, but he couldn't just stand there and say nothing while the doctor wiped his glasses for what must have been the fiftieth time. The doctor was in his early fifties, very tall, about six and a half feet, with an easy-going face and graying hair, and looked exactly what he was: a doctor at a crime scene. He had a vague resemblance to the singer Francesco Guccini, and seemed as much at ease in that parking lot as Francesco did on stage. He had dressed in great haste as usual: in addition, he had arrived home late from a reception and couldn't have gotten much sleep.

"No, but if *I* don't tell her . . . Poor thing. Poor things, both of them."

He seemed more concerned about the mother than the daughter. That was only natural: the mother was an old friend of his, who always spent at least a couple of weeks in Pineta every year. He probably hadn't seen the daughter much, just enough to recognize her. Whenever they went out together, the children (Arianna's daughter, Dr. Carli's son, and other young people from the area) went out separately.

Massimo was released from his predicament by the stentorian voice of Inspector Fusco, about whom he had decidedly mixed feelings.

He had talked about him once with Dr. Carli, as it happened, and they had found themselves in agreement that it wasn't humanly possible to find anything in Inspector Fusco (or Dr. Fusco as he liked to be called, being a graduate) that inspired the slightest sympathy. After the two men had concluded that Vinicio Fusco was prickly, arrogant, pig-headed, conceited and vain, the doctor had passed judgment:

"The man is like a book of jokes about Calabrians."

And whenever Massimo, who had entirely approved of this conclusion, thought about Fusco he couldn't help wondering if, thanks to rubbing shoulders with Rimediotti, he wasn't becoming a bit of a racist. He consoled himself with the thought that when he was at university in Pisa, a Sicilian friend of his, who could be accused of everything except making racial distinctions, had in a drunken moment drawn up "a profile of the perfect idiot": and among various other basic characteristics that Massimo couldn't remember, this person had to be an engineer, a supporter of Juventus, and a Calabrian.

Anyway, Inspector—or Dr.—Fusco had arrived just at the right moment. In a good mood, because he loved his work and liked doing it in front of an audience, he had come up behind the two of them, taking them by surprise, and boomed cheerfully, "So, Walter, tell me everything: age, sex, time, cause, any other business."

The doctor looked down at the tips of his shoes, put his hands together behind his back, and said, "Age nineteen, sex female, as if you needed a doctor to tell you that, time of death between two and five hours ago, no more, no less. Cause of death, strangulation. Any other business, the world is full of assholes."

Fusco took this full on. He had almost certainly forgotten that Carli knew her. He stood there for a moment, with his jaw jutting forward and his hands on his hips, then he resolved to get on with things to cancel out the fact that he'd made a fool of himself. He immediately began by screaming at the photographers that he wanted the prints before the morning was over, then focused his attention on a dark green Clio parked nearby, with its right-side wheels stuck in the mud.

"What about that?"

He went to the car, looked through the window, and assumed the expression of someone who understands everything. Then he pointed at one of the officers and beckoned him to approach.

Massimo watched in amusement as the officer, a young man as tall as a beanpole, strode up to the diminutive Fusco and stood to attention to receive his orders.

"At ease, Pardini," Fusco said, addressing the officer's chest. "That's the car belonging to the young man who found the body. The keys are still on the dashboard. Move it away from here, it's getting on my nerves."

"Excuse me, Inspector," the young man in question intervened. He had been waiting to be questioned, and now felt as if he was the center of attention.

Fusco raised his hand to silence him. "It's all right, son, while your car's being moved we can have a little chat. What time was it that you discovered the body?"

"There's something I have to tell you first. That—"

Fusco gave the young man a truculent look, one he had probably rehearsed for minutes on end, and stood with his hands on his hips. "Son, first you need to answer my questions. I know you have a hangover, so I'll repeat it slowly and maybe you'll understand. *What time was it that you discovered the body?*"

In the meantime Pardini had gotten in the car, adjusted the seat by moving it forward, turned the key in the ignition, and started the engine. The wheels skidded in the mud, but the car didn't move. Two other officers arrived, began pushing, and eventually managed to get the car out.

"About four, I'm sure of that."

"What position was she in?"

"She was inside the trash can, with her face sticking out. Like she was when we came back."

"I know, I know. And you went straight to the bar?"

"Not immediately. I waited a while until I was less dizzy, then when I felt better I left. I almost crashed my car getting there. A brand new Micra."

Fusco looked at the young man, the dark green Clio, the

young man again, then at the puddle in front of him, and, staring down at the mud, said, "What?"

"I said I waited a while then—"

"Stop!" Fusco yelled at the officers who had shifted the car by now, then looked up at the sky and moaned, "Shit!" He turned back angrily to the young man. "You could have told me before! A car with keys on the dashboard in the place where a body has been found, and I have it moved! Why? Because nobody tells me anything! What the hell do you have in that head of yours?"

"Look, Inspector," the young man said, clearly genuinely upset and even a little scared, "that's what I was trying to tell you before, but you interrupted me . . . "

Eyes open wide, the inspector put his hands back in his pockets. He looked at everyone present as threateningly as he could, then turned and walked away muttering audibly, "It's always your fault, Fusco. Oh, yes."

The young man said nothing, merely looked at Fusco's back with an expression that was starting to betray a certain lack of trust in the authorities.

Massimo and the doctor, who had both regained the semblance of a smile, exchanged knowing looks.

"Every time I see him in action I discover something new," the doctor said.

Then his face abruptly darkened again.

Partly out of curiosity, partly in an attempt to distract him for five more minutes, Massimo asked the doctor, "Can you explain one thing to me? When you said 'between two and five hours ago,' did you say that to be on the safe side, even though you may have a more specific time in mind, or did you really mean such a long interval?"

The doctor shook his head. "At the moment that's how it is, I can't say anymore," he replied without looking at Massimo. "To be more certain we'll need more tests, we'll need to determine the progress of the auricular or rectal temperature over time, examine the stomach contents if we know the exact time of her last meal, and then we can be more precise, but it all depends on when it happened. If death occurred not long ago, we can be very precise. However"—now he looked at Massimo—"I'm pretty sure the girl died about midnight, an hour more, an hour less. But I'll only be sure after . . . well, afterwards."

Fusco was coming back in their direction. He beckoned to the doctor, and as he waited for him to approach said loudly to Massimo and the young man, "You two, make sure you're available, I still have to interview you officially. I'll send for you in the afternoon."

"So now you have to go see Fusco and be questioned?"

By now the bar was empty, inside and outside. The people had all gone to the sea, there wouldn't be anybody about until six in the evening, at which time they would arrive in groups of two or three to have a flatbread and a beer on the way back from the beach. Then, from seven until such time as it pleased the Almighty, life would begin. Letting his thoughts wander, Massimo imagined the scenes he would soon be seeing, the people he would greet. Every night, there were guys with gym-trained bodies and improbably tanned girlfriends, men from Livorno wearing vests over their naked chests and big gold medallions, and women so gorgeous and smooth and trim they could only be high-class hookers, and Massimo often found himself thinking they were all different but all identical, and then, as always, was irrationally ashamed of himself for pigeon-holing such an interesting group.

Sometimes he was so curious about these people that he felt like going up to them and getting into conversation, just to see what kind of people they were. He'd actually done so some-times, and the experience hadn't really been worth it.

"Planet Earth calling Massimo. Come in, Massimo!"

Massimo gave a start. Aldo had been standing there with his hands around his mouth like a megaphone. Now he put them down and nodded at Massimo.

"What is it?"

"So now you have to go see Fusco?"

"Yes, in half an hour. Why?"

"Shouldn't he come here?"

Ampelio came to his aid. "Yes, he should. You're working. If he just wants to ask you a couple of questions he could come here without the hassle of you having to go there! Don't you think so?"

Massimo smiled and shook his head. "Grandpa, he has to interview me at the station so that someone can take down my statement. And if he did come here, can you imagine? In ten minutes, the whole town would know everything the inspector knows. More, in fact. And don't give me those martyred looks!"

"Well . . . " Pilade sprawled back on his chair, in the typical attitude of someone about to reveal something. He grabbed the pack of Stop cigarettes, took one out (how can you smoke something like that? Massimo always thought) and lit it as he started speaking, so that the cigarette between his lips bobbed up and down to the rhythm of the words. "You know the neat thing about this whole business, my dear Massimo? It's that the town already knows more than the inspector. Firstly, because Fusco is a fool"—all those present nodded in unison—"and secondly, because if something happens in this town, to someone from the town, then someone else must know something about it. Maybe someone who saw something but doesn't know what it meant. In my opinion, Massimo, Fusco should come to the bar and talk to all the people who drop in here, then go to see all the women in their homes, then go to the market, and so on. Nobody'll go straight to him. But,

I tell you, by the time I left home at ten past two my wife had already been on the phone for an hour and twenty minutes. And when I go home again you can be sure she'll be pounding my eardrums with the murder."

Massimo laughed. Pilade was right: the old women's brainstorming sessions were so fearsome that nobody would escape the deductions of all these would-be Miss Marples shut up at home telephoning everybody they knew.

Just as long as they don't accuse me, he thought.

THREE

N ame?"
"Massimo Viviani."
"Born?"
"Of course, or else I wouldn't be here."
"Would you mind telling me exactly where and when?"
"Pisa, February 5, 1969."
"Thank you. Profession?"
"Barman."

Massimo's bad mood at having to go to the police station had gotten significantly worse. He had waited almost an hour for the inspector (who he hoped was in the grip of a binding commitment of the intestinal kind) in a gloomy little room with a glass door, a photograph of President Ciampi, and a brochure on the usefulness and importance of bomb disposal experts. After reading it two or three times and looking for printing errors (not a single one, which was unusual) he had lit a cigarette and let his mind wander until the moment he was called. One of the three subordinates had come to fetch him and had showed him into his lord and master's office, unfortunately vacant as said lord and master was obviously still in the toilet.

The inspector had arrived only after fifteen intentional minutes, thus giving Massimo time to memorize the details of all the police uniforms from 1890 to the present day, as depicted on a poster that was the only concession to art in the room. If Fusco had questioned him about it, he would have been able to describe them all in reverse order. Instead of which the inspector lowered his clasped hands from in front of his face, placed them on the desk, and asked, "Could you tell me about the events of the morning of August 12?"

"Well, I got up about four. I took my car and arrived here in Pineta about ten before five."

"Right, you live in the city. Simone Tonfoni, the person who found the body, maintains that he entered your bar at 5.10. Can you confirm that?"

"Yes."

"After he entered, he says he phoned this station to report finding the body. The officer on duty at the switchboard thought it was a joke and hung up. Then . . . "

"Then I asked him to show me where the body was. We went to the parking lot, I saw the scene, went back to the bar and—"

"Please just answer my questions and don't interrupt," the inspector said calmly. "Did you phone the station at 5.20 A.M.?"

"Yes."

"Did you go back to the parking lot immediately after the phone call?" "Yes."

"Was the scene of the crime exactly as it had been the first time?"

"Yes."

"Did you wait for the police to arrive, without leaving the spot?"

"Yes."

"Are you sure about what you're telling me?"

"Yes."

"Is yes the only word you know?"

"No."

Fusco looked at him for a moment with a cow-like expression, then stood up silently from his chair (as he was an inspector, he had a chair on castors, whereas the other officers were allocated ordinary chairs without castors, and so to indulge in their frequent diversion of competing to see who could get from the waiting room to the filing cabinets on a chair the quickest, they were forced to use Fusco's, when he was out, of course) and went and placed himself in front of the window, turning his back on the room. There he stood, his hands behind his back, in a knowing posture. It struck Massimo that even this was something rehearsed over and over by Fusco, probably inspired by Chazz Palminteri in *The Usual Suspects*. Massimo found it amusing, this parody of an American cop. Blessed are the simple, he thought, for they shall inherit the kingdom of heaven and police stations on Earth.

He was about to ask if he could use the bathroom for a moment, but before he could the inspector asked, in a less formal tone of voice, "Did you know the victim, Signor Viviani?"

Massimo shifted on his chair to make himself more comfortable. "I may have seen her in the bar a few times, but I don't remember. I know her name was Alina Costa and that she lived in the building next to the Luna Rossa offices."

"Do you know if anyone knew her well?"

"No idea," Massimo said. "I didn't know her, I don't even know who she went around with. Dr. Carli knows her mother well, and I'm sure he knew her too, but only because she was her mother's daughter. You'd better ask him."

"How does the doctor happen to know Signora Costa?"

"She'd been the best friend of the woman who later became his wife, when he was at university. His wife forced all her dreadful friends on him before they were married, and made him keep seeing them afterwards. From what Dr. Carli says, Arianna Costa is the only decent person among those his wife allows him to see."

"How come? I mean, how come Signora Carli is so . . . "

The inspector couldn't find the right word, so Massimo kindly helped him out. "Selective? Domineering? Such a pain in the ass?"

"All three would do. Anyway how come?"

Massimo heaved a long, eloquent sigh. This was something he felt competent to speak about. Ever since he had started working as a barman on the coast, this kind of subject was a constant topic of conversation.

"Practically speaking, when the two of them met she had lots of money, whereas he, although he wasn't too badly off, wasn't all that well off either. So they had different habits, vacationed in different places, met different people. But while he would never have dreamed of taking her to his friends' homes to watch soccer matches, she started introducing him into her world. She took him to the Rotary Club, she took him to regattas, she took him to Forte dei Marmi, and so on. Along the same lines, if his friends phoned the house, she wouldn't put them through to him. I know that sounds very Victorian, but that's the way it is. She won't allow intruders into her gilded world."

Fusco had now turned and was leaning on the window sill with his hands on the edge. "And he lets her?"

Massimo leaned back in his chair and started to swing his legs slightly. "Obviously, it's not as bad as it sounds. To hear him tell it, he seems to live in a novel by Wodehouse, full of characters who don't do a stroke of work from morning to night and keep their brains under wraps for fear that they might get damaged, seeing that they don't have a lot there in the first place. It's not surprising he became friendly with Arianna Costa: she was the only person from his wife's circle who has any idea what's going on. She's a snob, but she's intelligent."

Fusco rose from the window sill. The conversation was obviously drawing to a close.

Thank God, Massimo thought. I have to rush to the bathroom or I'll do it in my pants.

"So, in conclusion, you can't tell me anything about the victim."

It wasn't a question, and Massimo didn't bother to reply. He was only waiting to be dismissed, given that his bladder was close to exploding, so he also stood up and walked toward the door. In a sudden fit of kindness, Fusco got to the door first and opened it for him. "Please. I really would like to know something about the victim."

Massimo, who had been about to go out, stopped in the doorway. He pretended to ponder the inspector's words, nodding slowly, then made as if to move and was again blocked by the inspector.

"Often, it's by finding out about the victim that we track down his murderer."

"I'm sure that's right. So can I—"

"Look, let me tell you something. But please, try to keep it to yourself."

Massimo resigned himself and leaned back against the doorpost. "That's getting harder by the minute. No, sorry, I was thinking of something else. Go on."

"The girl didn't show up for a date last night, but that was almost two hours before she was killed. We need to find out where she was. If you hear anything about it, don't tell anyone, come straight to me. Anything might be important. Goodbye, Signor Viviani."

When he left the station, Massimo set off on foot for the center of town, where the bar was located.

If she hadn't kept a date, he thought, that meant there were two possibilities. The first, that she had gone to the place where she was killed. The second . . . well, the second was that she was already dead. No, the hour of death ruled that out. But there was a second possibility all the same, he thought. The person who said they had a date with her might not have been telling the truth. Why? To cover for someone? Or to create an alibi for himself? I really don't know anything about these things, he thought.

A passing woman gave him a curious look, and only then did Massimo realize that he has been thinking aloud, talking to himself.

Massimo often talked to himself when he was thinking: a habit he had gotten into when he was revising for his exams in the first years of university. He would imagine that he had his professor physically there in front of him and would interact with him so realistically as to even exchange, for example, a few remarks about the weather. That was how he had discovered that, by pretending to present an argument to someone, the ideas came to him with greater clarity: it was like forcing his thoughts to travel at the right speed. All the same, he didn't like being noticed talking to himself on the street, so he didn't think about anything more until he got to the bar.

It was not until after two that the last couple of people left the bar, when Massimo had already started putting the chairs upside down on the tables and counting out loud. It was only to be expected: if a murder takes place in a seaside resort in the middle of summer, everybody talks about it. If you then happen to find yourself in the very bar whose owner discovered the corpse, it's party time. Every now and again someone, erroneously convinced that he had an original idea, would shout out over the voices of whichever group of debauchees he was with, "Hey, did you know it was Massimo who found the body this morning? Why don't you tell us how it happened? Come on . . . "

He had told it a dozen times, each time adding new details so that at least he didn't get too bored.

"Massimo, I can come tomorrow morning if you like, if you

want to get some sleep. Then I'll leave at noon and come back about six, six thirty. Is that okay?"

Tiziana, the girl who helped Massimo in the bar, was finishing sweeping while Massimo threw away the night's leftover appetizers. Tall, with good posture, a redhead as her name suggested, she had been hired by Massimo because she possessed two perfect attributes for working in a bar. Firstly, she wasn't clumsy. Secondly, she had beautiful breasts, which she concealed with little success inside tight-fitting sweaters or blouses with the buttons undone but knotted at the bottom. By now Massimo was used to it, but in the early days he had often found himself looking inadvertently at her chest as he spoke to her, unable to take his eyes off it, as if drawn there by a magnet, while continuing to talk as if everything was normal. Fortunately, she had laughed it off. The customers unconditionally approved of her presence, although Francesca Ferrucci, who had the tobacconist's opposite the bar, had once objected that basically it was unfair that the spectacle behind the counter reserved for the female public was not on the same level as that for the male public. That had made Massimo feel very ugly, and for some time he had served the woman a deliberately undrinkable type of coffee.

"Thanks, Tiziana, that'd be great. I'm not too tired, but I would like to sleep in tomorrow. Aren't you going out with Marchino tonight?"

That was a gaffe, as he immediately realized from the renewed vigor with which Tiziana continued her sweeping.

"Something wrong?"

"Kind of."

"I'm sorry."

"Oh it's nothing. The usual story. By the way, I almost forgot. This afternoon, while you were away, O.K. came in looking for you. He said it was important, and that he'd come back tomorrow."

"The usual story" really was the usual story. Like many young women after a certain age, Tiziana was determined to get married. And like many young men when they heard the word marriage, her paramour Marchino tended to change the subject. Sometimes one of the two insisted too much, and they would quarrel and pretend for half a day that they didn't know each other. Then everything went back to being the way it was before.

"O.K.? That's strange. He never asks for anything. I wonder what he wants. Well, goodnight."

"'Night."

FOUR

The alarm clock. Is that the alarm clock? Shit. All right, I'll get up. Now, my slippers. Where are my slippers? Nice slippers . . . Oh, thank God. Fuck, what a horrible taste in my mouth, it's like I've eaten a kilo of dust. Coffee, now. Thank God I've got coffee. Who was it who invented coffee? He must be a cousin of the genius who invented the bed. Nobel Prizes for both of them. For them, and for the person who invented Nutella. In church, instead of the statue of San Gaspare. At least then we'd see a bit more sincere devotion. All right, let's have a shower and then I'll go.

Wide awake after his shower, Massimo pushed open the glass door and walked into the bar. He hadn't seen Grandpa Ampelio or the three other musketeers outside at the tables.

Here was the explanation: they were inside, and had been waiting eagerly for him. Sitting at the table next to theirs, with both his elbows leaning on the edge of it, was a man who could best be described as a disaster zone. He was almost bald, but what little hair he still had was shoulder-length. He had a long beard, and in spite of the heat was wearing a padded black jacket and long pants. To complete the picture, the fingers of his right hand were missing, leaving only the thumb. In his left hand he was holding a cup of coffee, examining it with a doubtful air, almost as if wondering if it might not be risky to drink something non-alcoholic like this in the morning on an empty stomach.

"Hello everyone."

"Nice to see you, son," Ampelio greeted him. "We've been waiting for you for two hours. I guess you were scared they'd take away your pillow and you were hugging it for safekeeping."

"Hello, O.K.," Massimo said, going behind the counter. "I heard you were looking for me. Is it something important?"

Obviously it was important, Massimo thought. O.K. was so reserved that days might pass before he'd even think about speaking to anyone. The son of a fisherman and a fisherman's wife (which is a profession in itself, and not one of the most restful), Remo Carlini had been a peaceable, curious child who devoted all his waking hours to learning the secrets of nature. Many questions had come into his mind, such as "How long will it take this lizard to die after I've cut off its head?" "Why don't cats fall on their feet if you tie a weight to their tails?" and "What happens if I pick up that cone-shaped metal object?" The answer to this last question—sometimes the object explodes in your hand—had deprived him of four fingers, and the death of his parents a few years later had deprived him of board and lodgings. So Remo Carlini—known as O.K. because his right hand, equipped only with a thumb as it was, seemed always to be signaling that everything was fine, in a gesture typical of American films of the 1960s—was the only homeless person in Pineta. He ate what he could find in trash cans, especially those behind restaurants, and sometimes went into a bar and ordered a drink, which he paid for with coins picked up on the street. He didn't beg, and he didn't ask for company, except for the two or three childhood friends of his who were still alive.

In the early days of the bar, Massimo had noticed O.K. looking for leftovers in the trash can, and had wondered what he could do to give him something—he had been told that O.K. didn't accept charity and that it was practically impossible to talk to him. In the end he had gotten into the habit of taking the leftover sandwiches of the day and putting them neatly on a little tray that he then wrapped with the greatest care and placed on the top of the trash can. O.K. had noticed, and from then on if he met Massimo on the street he would greet him silently by pretending to take off his hat. Today must have been only the fourth or fifth time in three years that he had heard his voice.

"Oh, yes, it's very important. That girl in the trash can, right? She was put there later."

"What do you mean?" Massimo asked, having understood nothing at all of O.K.'s confused speech. "Later than what?"

"Listen, but I mean, really listen. You found the dead girl, right?"

"Right."

"Good. You found her at five fifty, right? Ampelio told me. But yesterday was Saturday, and the restaurants didn't have any leftovers. So by last night I was really starving. I looked in all the trash cans, everywhere, nothing. So I went to the pine wood, where people have picnics, maybe they'd left something. But there was nothing, even there. Nothing, got it? No chicken meat, no girl meat. Do you understand?"

I understand, I understand, Massimo thought.

"Goodbye then. You tell the police. Tell that idiot who tried to arrest me for vagrancy last year."

So that was why he came here. Massimo remembered hearing about that. It was understandable if O.K. didn't trust the police.

"Wait, sorry. What time was this?"

"Oh, yes. It was four thirty."

"By what watch?" Del Tacca asked dubiously. "Your gold Rolex?"

"No, the one I was given by that whore your mother, I like it so much I always keep it in the bank," O.K. replied without skipping a beat. "I saw the time on the clock at the disco, the green one that flashes. You can see it from all over."

He took his coffee, knocked it back in one go, stood up, and left the bar with his usual poise.

"It's true," said Aldo. "The laser clock at the Imperiale. You can even see it from the beach. So, let's recap: the girl is killed between midnight and three, right?"

"Right," Massimo replied, then in a loud voice, "Hello, doctor!"

"Hello."

Dr. Carli closed the door that O.K. had left open, waved a greeting at the four old-timers, who were all now engrossed in their newspapers, walked straight to the counter, and sat down on a stool.

"Could I have a sweet aperitif, please?"

"No."

"Excuse me?"

"No, you can't. It's a mental aberration, having an aperitif at lunchtime. Especially an alcoholic one. You drink on an empty stomach, then you go out with your senses already dulled a little, you go from a temperature of seventy-five inside, with air conditioning, to a hundred degrees out on the sidewalk, it hits you, and you collapse on the ground. I mean, sorry to point this out, but you are a doctor."

His curiosity aroused, the doctor looked at Massimo and decided to play along with him. "So what do you suggest, master?"

"At lunchtime, nothing. At dinner, maybe some sparkling wine or champagne."

"Sweet?"

Massimo put his hand on his chest and feigned a slight heart attack.

With an anxious expression, the doctor moved closer to the counter. "Why? Isn't it possible? Has it become illegal?"

"No, it's just that sweet sparkling wine isn't drunk as an aperitif. Apart from the fact that, except for Asti, sweet sparkling wines are usually crap, you need something to whet the appetite, not kill it. A good brut has the right characteristics, a sickly sweet sparkling wine doesn't."

The doctor seemed to weigh up this explanation, then resigned himself to a glass of mineral water. He seemed a lot more relaxed than he had been the morning he had seen the body. For him, the worst must be over. He looked around with a disinterested air, walked up behind Ampelio, who had opened the newspaper at random at a full-page article about supernovas, glanced at it and said, "Massimo knows his stuff when it comes to wines, doesn't he? Almost as much as Signor Griffa here."

"Almost," Aldo agreed solemnly.

"I'm no connoisseur, but we don't need a news commentator to figure out what you were discussing. It's no sin. You don't have to stop when I come in. What do you think, I'm going to tell Fusco?"

"All right, you caught us with our pants down," Massimo said. "Is there any news?"

"What makes you think I'd know? O.K. didn't talk to me."

How the hell is it that people always know what's going on? Massimo thought. What do they have in their homes, satellite receivers?

"Listen, we'll tell you what O.K. told us . . . "

"That seems only fair, and I'll tell you what Fusco told me."

Four timeworn necks craned towards the counter.

"I don't believe it!" Ampelio said. "Has he found something?"

"But keep it to yourselves as long as possible, please."

Believe us, the four faces said, while Massimo's face made an effort to keep as deadpan as possible. The important thing, when you gossip, is to maintain a formal structure. The person spreading the gossip has to demand the maximum secrecy, and the listeners have to grant it. Obviously, they'll broadcast the news as widely as they can later. It's just a matter of time. If someone says, "Keep it to yourselves as long as possible," he doesn't mean "Tell it to the fewest possible people," but "Resist for at least a little while before coming out with it, that way it'll be harder to trace it back to me."

"Fusco had the trash can searched, and found Alina's cell phone. He's been able to read all the texts in its memory and . . . "

" . . . and discovered that she had a date."

The doctor looked at Massimo and raised an eyebrow.

The rest of the chorus turned their necks like a ballet of periscopes toward

Massimo, who had gone around to the other side of the counter to cut the focaccia into sandwiches for lunchtime.

"Fusco told me the other day, after he questioned me."

And you didn't tell us anything, said the faces of the old man. Shame on you.

"But I don't know who the date was with. He kept that to himself."

"I'm just getting to that," the doctor said. "The inspector discovered that she sent three texts, one to a girl, and two to a boy. She also received four messages, all from the same boy as before. In addition, she spoke on the phone for the last time with a girl, the same one she'd sent a text to."

"And what did these texts say?" Massimo asked.

"What the hell are these texts anyway?" Ampelio asked, feeling that he was losing out on the best part of it.

"Texts," Dr. Carli, "are written messages that are sent through cell phones, computers or even your home phone if you have the right device. The kids use them a lot, partly because sending them is cheaper than calling. And besides, it's fashionable."

Ampelio made a somewhat disparaging gesture with his chin and grunted, "The times we live in! When I was young, fortunately, it was fashionable to fuck . . . "

"Anyway," the doctor went on, ignoring these Ampelian regrets, "the first of the three messages told the girl that Alina might be going out to dinner with a guy. In the second, meant for the boy, she asked him if he was free for dinner. She also said they had to talk. In the third she asked him to pick her up from her place at ten, because her parents were out. As it happens, Arianna and her husband were at the same party I was at. We spent quite a while scrounging food from the Marquis and Marchioness Calvelli."

"And the messages received?" Massimo asked, all the while imagining the doctor in a tuxedo, smiling at old Marchioness Ermenegilda Calvelli-Storani and murmuring under his breath, "Ihopeyoucroaksoonyoufatpig" as he kissed her hand.

"All four are from the boyfriend. In the first he confirms the date. In the second he tells her he'll wait outside her building. In the third he asks her where she is. In the fourth he tells her to go to hell. Prophetic, really."

The doctor broke off, and took another cigarette from the pack. He lit it and was silent for a few moments. Nobody dared to speak.

"In between, there's the conversation with the girlfriend. Fusco's interviewing her now. Anyway, I have to go to the morgue. But as I'm here, I might as well eat here first. My wife isn't waiting for me today."

"Where did you leave her?" Del Tacca asked cheerfully. "With her lover?"

"In Saturnia, at the spa. She goes there every three or four months, to do God knows what. But when she comes back, she feels better, she's actually calmer, more relaxed."

And you're calmer too, Massimo thought, but you're ashamed of admitting it to yourself. Massimo's hadn't had these problems with his ex-wife. She'd let him do whatever he liked, as long as he didn't cheat on her. Actually, she was the one who'd cheated on him. The bitch.

"That's because she doesn't see you for a week," Del Tacca said in the same cheerful tone. "Then she comes back, sees you again, and falls at your feet. Some things have an effect on a beautiful woman like your wife. Though God knows why she insists on coming back . . . "

"I don't know, I just appreciate it. Massimo, can you make me a sandwich on foccaccia, whatever kind you like?"

"Just give me a moment. I have to make a couple of phone calls first."

Massimo went out the back, took the phone from the wall, and dialed the number of the police station. A voice with a Sicilian accent said, "Pineta Police, hello."

"Hello, this is Massimo Viviani. I'd like to speak with Dr. Fusco."

He couldn't help it, it had just come out like that. Fortunately the switchboard operator played along with him.

"A witness is currently helping Dr. Fusco with his inquiries into the Costa homicide. Would you like me to inform the doctor immediately?"

"Yes, please." In order to maintain the level of bureaucratic language, he added, "Without further ado."

A brief silence, then Fusco's voice reached his ear, sounding quite conspiratorial in tone. "Hello?"

"Hello, Inspector. Listen, I have to talk to you. This morning in the bar a person gave me some information that may be important—"

"Concerning the case?" the inspector cut in brusquely.

"Yes. Practically speaking—"

"Not a word on the phone. Come straight here." And he hung up.

Fusco really did seem over-excited.

I wonder who he's talking to, Massimo asked himself, even though he already had an idea. Dr. Carli had said he'd been interviewing the girlfriend. It was extremely likely he was now talking to the boyfriend Alina had sent the texts to.

He called Tiziana on her cell phone, but there was no reply. She'd probably gone to bed and couldn't hear the phone. What to do now? He couldn't leave the bar unattended, and in order to close he'd have to throw out the old-timers. He went back in and called Aldo over.

"Aldo, Fusco wants me at the station right now. What time do you have to be at the restaurant?"

"About six. Do you want me to mind the bar?"

"That'd be great. You know where I keep everything, more or less. I'll be back in an hour, two at the most. Don't give my grandpa all he asks for, or he'll feel sick. And don't, I repeat don't, let him get at the ice cream."

"Don't worry."

"Thanks. See you later."

"See you soon," the doctor said. "But what about my sandwich?"

"Oh, yes, of course. I'll make it for you before I go. Salt beef, lemon, grilled zucchini, and dill."

"Sounds good. All right."

"It is good, trust me. Even if you didn't like it I'd make it anyway."

While Massimo was slicing, Rimediotti asked the doctor, "That car, do we know whose it is?"

"Yes, it's Alina's. It got stuck in the mud near the trash can. It's clear the murderer didn't want to stay there too long, so he left on foot, either through the pine wood or along the street."

"What was it, a green Clio?"

"Yes, a new Clio. Just like mine. Arianna told me she wanted to buy the girl a car, something simple to drive, and asked me what the Clio was like. I told her I was happy with mine, so she got one. Three months ago. It seems like a hundred years."

"Have they done the post mortem yet?"

The doctor looked down at Pilade and nodded slowly. "I just finished it. I can't tell you anything. Thanks, Massimo," he said, taking the sandwich, "and can you give me also an iced tea, please?"

"Help yourself, I'm going to phone the girl."

He went and dialed the number of Tiziana's cell phone. Nothing. He tried her home number. At the sixth ring, a voice said, "Hi, this is Tiziana and I'm not in. Leave a message and I'll call you back."

"This is your employer Massimo Viviani speaking. Binding commitments to the civil authorities are taking me away from my business. Come here as soon as you can, I'll pay you over-time until six."

He went back, grabbed his billfold, and pointed to the half-eaten sandwich on the plate. "Don't you want the rest?"

"No, it's good, but my stomach's tight."

"Worried?"

The doctor looked at Massimo in a cow-like way, then nodded again. Stupid question, Massimo thought, look what I just asked him. He opened the door and left without saying good-bye.

Damn. Can't breathe in this heat. Look at me, for that pain in the ass Fusco I'm going to catch the mother of all sunstrokes, damn him, and his mother for good measure.

This was all Massimo was able to think as he walked to the station.

To keep cool, he took a slightly longer way around, through the pine wood. Mechanically, he took out a cigarette, but then it struck him he wouldn't enjoy it in this heat, so he put it back in the pack and carried on walking.

As he walked, lost in thought, he looked down on the ground and catalogued the refuse strewn through the pine wood. "A coke carton . . . paper from a sandwich . . . one of mine, yes . . . good boys . . . a pen . . . a condom wrapper . . . how do they manage it? . . . I'd be scared . . . plus you get pine needles in your ass, which must hurt . . . leftover rigatoni . . . that's worse . . . rigatoni in tomato sauce to the sea, my God . . . some people even bring fish stew and ceramic plates with them . . . and wine . . . Florentines, of course . . . they really are the limit, anybody would think they're getting ready for a siege, they bring everything . . . bread, ham, flippers and glasses, a rubber crocodile 'for the kid,' loads of food . . . there must be ten a year that drown . . . it's amazing they don't die of congestion right here in the pine wood . . . at least if I talk to myself here there's nobody to hear me . . . "

All the same, he fell silent.

*

After leaving the pine wood, he had only another hundred yards to walk to reach the station, but it was enough to bathe him in sweat. He couldn't bear even the thought of being sweaty: it made him ill at ease.

He walked into the station, sat down on a banquette, put his legs up on it, and settled down to a long wait.

Instead of which, much to his surprise, Fusco came out of his office and beckoned him inside. There, obviously in the process of being questioned, was a girl of about seventeen in a green top that served only to emphasize her breasts and an orange micro skirt—dressed like that, she looked like Cher's granddaughter—and a slightly older boy.

The boy was of medium height, so tanned that his teeth seemed fluorescent. He looked as if he hadn't slept for several hours. In spite of the air conditioning, both of them were dripping with sweat, and the girl had clearly been crying only a short time ago.

The inspector, on the other hand, seemed perfectly at ease. He sat down and motioned with his hand for Massimo to do the same.

"Well, Signorina, I don't need you anymore for now. Officer Pardini will ask you to dictate your statement and sign it. I must ask you, however, not to leave town, I might need to speak with you again. When were you planning to return home, Signorina Messa?"

The girl sniffed and said, "I don't know, in a week, I think . . . but if you need me I can stay, I can even stay all summer, I . . . I'd do anything . . . " and she started to cry, silently. The boy wasn't looking at her, it seemed he was doing everything he could not to burst into tears too, although he seemed more scared than grief-stricken. And with good reason, Massimo thought. The girl managed to control herself and gave him a questioning look, and he made a jerky movement with one hand to tell her that everything was all right. She looked at him again and, by signs, made it clear that she'd be waiting for him. He made a sign to say no, then lifted one hand in an uncertain attempt to reassure her. Massimo started to feel ill at ease and was about to tell Fusco that he would come back later, but the inspector looked at him and gestured to him to remain seated. He called Officer Pardini and had the girl shown out, then stood up and asked in a low voice, "You have something for me?"

"Well, you know, O.K. dropped by this morning. He told me something that might be important."

"And that would be?"

"That he searched in that trash can at four-thirty in the morning, looking for something to eat. He says the girl wasn't there yet."

"Four-thirty in the morning. How can he be sure of the time?"

"He saw it on the laser clock."

"The laser clock?"

"Yes, the one at the Imperiale."

"Strange." Fusco sat down and started drumming with a pencil on the desk. "Really strange. In other words, the girl was put there between four-thirty and five in the morning. That's a very narrow window of time. All right. There's something else. Since the girl was killed between midnight and one, and the medical report is precise about this, that obviously means the murder was committed somewhere at least four or five hours by car from the trash can. Which means the whole of Tuscany, Umbria, Liguria and part of Lazio."

Yes, and the rest of Italy too, Massimo thought. What kind of car do you have, a used Trabant with a rear trailer full of paving stones?

"Well," the inspector said, "I'm most grateful, and I'll let you get back to your work. First though, go to see Officer

Tonfoni and sign the statement you forgot to sign last time. Have a good afternoon."

Waiting for him outside was not only the usual wave of hot air, but the girl. She had stopped crying. She came up to Massimo as he was walking quickly toward the pine wood, longing for its coolness.

"Excuse me, can I ask you something?"

"Go ahead."

Massimo slowed down. In spite of this the girl, who wasn't very tall, had to walk quickly to keep up with him. She walked on high heels with an ease that impressed him. She was little more than a child, but had the overall look and carriage of a model, much more so than the twenty-five-year-old bimbos who consumed the air and the potato chips in his bar at aperitif time. His ex-wife, the bitch, couldn't walk on high heels: once when they had gone to the theater she had bought a pair of high-heeled shoes for the occasion—"You'll see, Massimo, how well they go with that red dress with the low cut jacket"— and the undeniable elegance of the ensemble when she was still had been spoiled by her unsteady, uncoordinated gait as soon as she started walking, like a car with manual gears driven by an American.

"That inspector . . . do you know him well?"

"Not very well," he replied. "He comes into my bar."

The girl looked at Massimo. "What kind of man is he?"

"I don't know . . . "

The girl looked at him again. She had green eyes, and her make-up, which had run everywhere because of her crying, made them stand out in a startling way. They seemed to be melting in the heat.

Massimo decided to be honest. "Basically, a bit of an asshole."

They had just entered the pine wood, silently. The girl looked at the ground, then turned aside, came to a halt, and began crying, also silently. Highly embarrassed, Massimo looked around and saw a bench. He sat the weeping girl down on it, hoping she would soon stop. He opened the pack of cigarettes and lit one, just to have something to do.

Sniffing, the girl said something that Massimo didn't understand.

"I'm sorry?"

"Bruno's the one."

"The boy who was with the inspector?"

"They were supposed to go out together yesterday."

Massimo amused himself for a moment with the image of Fusco waiting impatiently outside a restaurant with a big bunch of flowers, then returned to reality.

The girl looked around, then asked Massimo, "Could I have a cigarette?"

"Sure."

He handed her one, and she gave him a tentative smile.

"How do you know Alina and your friend were supposed to go out together?"

"He isn't my friend, he's my brother." A drag on the cigarette, followed by a pause. "Alina phoned me yesterday. She told me she was having dinner with someone, but she didn't say who. Then I asked her if this person was her boyfriend, and she said, 'In a way . . . ' I asked her if he was anyone I knew, and she said no, I definitely didn't know him."

She had stopped crying now, but not sniffing. She took out a handkerchief, blew her nose, and threw it away with a gesture that was starting to suggest practice.

All this while, Massimo had said nothing. Inside himself, he kept repeating, "It'snoneofyourbusinessit'snoneofyourbusinessit'snone . . . " To overcome the temptation. He was starting to wonder what he was doing in this situation, and why he was so curious about the whole thing.

I've spent so much time with those old guys, he thought, I'm becoming an old gossip myself. Come on, Massimo, mind your own business and go back to the bar, you have work to do.

"So why do you think it was your brother?" he asked finally, while the implausible but appropriate image of a stadium scoreboard appeared in his head, all lit up with the words *Temptation 3672 – Massimo 0*.

Slowly, the girl nodded. "Last night Bruno got a text from Alina on his cell phone. It said 'At ten outside my building?' and a smile. I know because I read it."

"Did your brother let you read it?"

"No, I snuck a look while he was in the bathroom. I know I shouldn't have, but I . . . " She broke off, looked Massimo straight in the eyes and said, with sudden frankness, "I didn't want him to go out with Alina."

Ah, Massimo thought.

"Sorry," he said, "I know this is none of my business," ("Liar!" flashed up on the scoreboard) "but why?"

The girl was about to answer when, announced by a rustle of leaves, a woman of about fifty appeared in the little clearing in front of the bench. She was as fat as a Sumo wrestler, and had a Yorkshire terrier on a lead. She stopped, panting, next to a tree and gave Massimo a distinctly unpleasant look that probably meant "That's disgusting, he must be twenty years older than her."

The girl looked at Massimo again and said, "Shall we go somewhere else?"

The woman was still giving them dirty looks, while her pint-sized dog performed a ridiculous little pee on a bush, from which Massimo imagined a Great Dane emerging, grabbing it in its jaws and carrying it away, like in *A Fish Called Wanda*.

"All right, come with me. How about an ice cream?" If he was going to be taken for a pedophile, Massimo thought, he might as well do it properly.

He stood up. As they walked away, he turned to look at the fat woman and, making sure the girl wasn't watching, smiled and made a gesture like a car accelerator, as if to say, "And after that I'll fuck her." The fat woman turned red.

Ten silent minutes later, they were sitting at a table in the shade outside the bar. Massimo had deliberately chosen the table farthest from the one where the old-timers were sitting, pretending to play cards and laughing. Aldo came out, still playing the barman. He placed himself behind the girl, cleared his throat discreetly, and asked in a prim voice, "What can I get your Highness?"

"You can go to hell to start with, and when you've done that, you can bring me an iced tea. What would you like?"

"A Coke, please."

Aldo gave a slight nod of approval and went away.

"Cigarette?"

"No, thanks. There are people here. My parents don't know I smoke."

"Sorry if I get straight back to the point, but why didn't you want your brother . . . "

The girl passed her hands through her hair, and a faraway look came into her eyes.

For a moment Massimo was afraid she was going to tell him it was none of his business, then get up and leave. And she wouldn't have been completely wrong, of course.

"Don't think I'm speaking ill of Alina, but . . . the fact is, when she was alive she was very independent, very bright, I mean . . . "

I understand, Massimo thought. When she was alive, she was a bit of a whore.

"She used to tell me about her boyfriends, what she did, where they took her . . . Nothing wrong with that, it was her business, but I didn't want her to make a fool of my brother.

They'd slept together once, last summer. It didn't mean anything to her. He was a friend, it had happened, and that was it . . . But he was enthralled by her. He'd phone her at least three or four times every day, if she went to the disco he'd go too, he didn't leave her alone for a second. She'd talk to him, at parties they'd slip away and come back after an hour, they'd share a towel on the beach. I think she liked having such a devoted admirer, but every now and again, when they weren't together, she'd go with other guys. I know because I saw her. She told me there was nothing between her and Bruno, they were just friends, and she'd made it clear to him that that's all they were. They liked being together. But I wanted him to get her out of his head. They started meeting in secret, without telling me. And now she's dead and I'm here . . . " (sob) "acting the fool and . . . " (another sob and a trembling of the chin) "and I don't even know what I feel worse about . . . "

She bowed her head, but then immediately looked up again. Her eyes were watery, but she had managed not to cry this time. Massimo thought it might be best to send her home as soon as possible.

"Do your parents know anything about this?"

"My parents . . . They don't know anything about anything. That's why I'm afraid to go home now. I mean, I can't go home and tell them what's happening. You have no idea.. They'd pass out."

Unless Fusco has already told them, in which case they've already passed out, Massimo thought. I hope you have your keys with you, or you'll have to sleep on the doormat.

"Maybe it's best if you do go home. Whatever happens, and there's no reason to suppose anything will happen, it's best if your parents hear about it from you. Trust me."

The girl kept her eyes down for a moment, then nodded tentatively. She stood up—revealing to Massimo the deep canyon of her cleavage, trapped within her green top—put her chair back in place and walked away. After a few steps, she turned and smiled.

"By the way, my name's Giada."

"Nice name. Mine's Massimo."

Aldo arrived with the poise of an English butler, put the drinks down on the table, and stood aside with his hands behind his back.

"Your Highness is served."

"Perfect timing, as usual."

"I'm sorry, your Highness, you told me to go to hell, but I wasn't familiar with the place and had a hard time finding it. I guess you know hell better than I do, this business is yours after all."

"Thanks, anyway. What on earth are those idiots laughing about inside?"

"They've been discussing the fact that your friend was young. They were wondering if she mightn't be too young to grasp certain things. In a metaphorical sense, of course."

"I can imagine. I'm coming inside now anyway, thanks for everything."

He went back into the bar, to be greeted by Grandpa Ampelio, grinning knowingly.

"Well?"

"What's that stain?"

"What stain?"

"That stain on your pants."

"Looks like ice cream to me. Must be old."

"Yes, yes, it's old." He turned to Aldo. "I'm damned if I'm going to leave the bar to you again, you and the rest of the retirement community here."

"It seems you don't like old people that much," Del Tacca said. "Obviously you prefer young flesh."

"Yes," Ampelio cut in. "You're a piece of work, aren't you?

Running after sixteen-year-olds now, with all the beautiful women there are around here. If only your grandma knew . . . "

"Grandpa, if Grandma Tilde knew half the things I see you do, say and eat here every day, you'd need the fire department to help you get back into your apartment."

Ignoring the threat, Ampelio put the cards in order.

"Anyway," Aldo said, "you've been having all the fun today."

Resistance was futile. If he kept pretending that everything was normal and didn't change the subject, they would continue making fun of him all day. Massimo sat down and began.

"All right, the name of the girl who was with me is Giada Messa. I met her at the station, she was there with her brother Bruno, who's the boy that got the last text from Alina's cell phone. The girl snuck a look at the text, it said he should come to Alina's place at ten, to go out to dinner."

"Dinner at ten?" Ampelio cut in. "How the world has changed. In my house they'd have gone without. When I was their age . . . "

"They know what happened when you were their age, because you're all the same age, plus I don't give a damn. Now will you all shut up and let me speak, or I'll finish tomorrow. The boy told his sister he got to Alina's place at nine-fifty and waited there until eleven-thirty. That much is fact. The rest is opinion. The girl says Alina and the brother had a thing going, I don't know enough to say if that's true or not. She's convinced it is. She also said that she didn't like it because—"

"Because when she was alive," Aldo said, "this Alina Costa may have been barely old enough to drive a car, but they say she'd already handled quite a few gear sticks."

Massimo looked at him for a moment.

"My God, how small this town is," Del Tacca said indifferently.

"I heard it from P.G., the guy who works at the Ara Panic."

The gleaming lights of the Ara Panic, the disco frequented by all those who thought they were cooler than everybody else, lit up the sky over a vast stretch of the sea front, all the way to the city. Summer and winter, a long line of deserters from the beach parked their unearned Mercedes at a forbidden angle to the curb, crowded to the ropes in front of the entrance, and submitted themselves hopefully or proudly to the scrutiny of other idiots hired by the establishment to grant admission only to the glossiest specimens, while inside, the volume of the music was so loud that it turned whatever brains those present still possessed to mush. The Druids who officiated at the ritual of selection were known as bouncers, and P.G., whose full name was Piergiorgio Neri, was one of the boldest representatives of this privileged caste. Thirty years old according to his birth certificate, with a deep tan, black hair that glinted in the sun, a depilated and overdeveloped chest that bulged beneath his tight-fitting, artfully ripped T-shirts, thirty-two shiny teeth, and a goatee beard dyed a charming shade of purple, P.G. aroused a wide range of reactions in the holidaymakers, from being worshipped as a totem by all the high school kids to provoking a rapid sign of the cross from the widow Falaschi.

"Handsome guy too. When did he tell you that?"

"Last night, at the restaurant. He has dinner there every night before he goes to the disco. He didn't eat much and drank water. Poor guy only ever drinks water. He was talking with two of his friends, and he said that the girl who died often went to the Ara Panic. He said last summer she spent more time on the couch than on the dance floor."

"And of course you just happened to overhear everything."

"Yes, I did, because he talks even louder than Ampelio. It must be because he's used to being surrounded by all that noise, but when he talks you can hear him all over the restaurant. One time, this guy sitting at the next table who looks like a hit man for the Russian Mafia gets pissed off and asks him, 'Don't you ever speak quietly?' And he comes straight back at him, 'Yes, when I fuck.' I've never seen anything like it. This guy comes right up to within an inch of his nose, looks him straight in the eyes for a few seconds and says very, very calmly, 'And what do you do when they kick you in the ass, cry?' I can tell you, ever since then, he's been like a lamb. Anyway, we were talking about Alina. P.G. also said that he hadn't seen her yet this summer, either at the disco or anywhere else."

"In my opinion he fucked her too," Rimediotti said, nodding sagely. "The man's a lecher. They say he once got a sixteen-year-old girl pregnant and made her have an abortion. I was told that by Zaira, whose grandson works at the Imperiale."

(Another basic rule, when sticking your nose into the business of people you've never seen or known, is to back up your statements with specific references to people or, better still, the relatives of people whose knowledge of the subject is guaranteed by some connection or other with the person in question. This makes even the most utter bullshit sound reassuringly logical.)

"I think we're getting off the track here," Del Tacca said. "Basically, P.G. isn't involved, so let's stick to the facts. They say this girl, God rest her soul, was a smart cookie, right? That makes sense to me. What doesn't make sense to me is something else." He sipped at his Campari to prolong the suspense. "Right, Massimo?"

"Possibly. If you tell me what it is, maybe it won't make sense to me either."

"No, no, trust me, it'll make sense to you. You've had this bar for two years, and in all that time you've been fucking us around. You're always getting involved in other people's business, I'd like to know why you should care less, you tell me if the man ever did you any harm . . . And now here you are, holding court! And before that you were talking for an hour with a girl you don't even know and you left the bar unattended. Am I right? So, since you don't know anybody in this case, can you tell me why. If there is a why."

Massimo crossed his legs, folded his arms, and looked at Del Tacca.

For the whole afternoon, he had been trying not to think about it. It's none of your business, he thought again. But since he wasn't capable of not thinking about it, he might as well give up.

"There is a reason. I saw Fusco. I saw the boy. I heard what the doctor said about the text messages. Fusco has put two and two together, and has found his culprit. Logical. Quick. An excellent result."

"I don't believe it," said Aldo. "An idiot like Fusco can't even solve a crossword, and now he has a murder dumped on his doorstep and he solves it in two days flat. Mind you, with the facts he's managed to put together, I'd have solved it too."

"In what sense?" Massimo asked.

"In the sense that I'd have identified the culprit. I mean, that boy." Aldo stood up from the table, went to the beer keg and filled his glass to the brim, talking all the while. "It isn't like in detective stories. There's the motive, there's the opportunity, there's the evidence. Everything makes sense."

"The two of you are idiots. You'd have both been wrong."

"Just listen to him," Rimediotti said. "Who else could it have been?"

"That, I don't know. But not Bruno Messa. Absolutely not."

There was a moment's silence. Then Ampelio laughed smugly, took his stick and pointed it at the other old men. "Look how they've all fallen for it. Massimo, as soon as you've stopped talking bullshit, can you make me a coffee?"

"I'm not joking, and I'm not talking bullshit. Let's see if I can make this any clearer. I'm absolutely certain that Bruno Messa, the young guy who's in Fusco's office right now, didn't kill Alina Costa. Unfortunately, I'm not in a position to prove it in any way that'd be admissible in a court of law."

This time the effect was miraculous. The four of them turned to look at him as if they were one old man.

"And how—" Del Tacca began, but was interrupted by Massimo.

"I have no intention of telling you guys anything. Besides, we can't be sure that Fusco will arrest the boy. He might not. Agreed, with the evidence he has at the moment he'd be an idiot not to, but nothing from him would surprise me."

"Excuse me, but in that case what are you planning to do?"

"If he doesn't arrest him, nothing. It's none of my business. If he does arrest him, I'll try to explain what I think. In the meantime, you guys . . . "—he realized the uselessness of what he was about to say, which was why he corrected himself— " . . . tell the fewest people possible."

SIX

"'Did She Have a Date with her Killer?
by Pericle Bartolini

"'Pineta: Alina Costa, the young woman brutally murdered in the early hours of Sunday morning, had a date with a friend, B. M., eighteen years old, the night she was killed. A date she did not keep, according to B. M. But the investigators have a different version. Yesterday, after an interrogation lasting more than four hours, Public Prosecutor Aurelio Bonanno officially placed the young man under investigation. His situation appears dire. According to the officer leading the investigation, Inspector Vinicio Fusco of the Pineta police, a reconstruction of the killer's movements is compatible with the period of time (between nine- thirty on Saturday evening and six on Sunday morning) for which the young man is not able to supply an alibi. According to pathologist Dr. Walter Carli, the murder took place between midnight and one in the morning. Subsequently, according to a number of witnesses, the body of the unfortunate young woman was transported between four-thirty and five-thirty in the morning to the place where she was found by S. T., nineteen years old, a third-year student at Leonardo Da Vinci Technical High School.'"

It was about eleven in the morning, and Rimediotti's high-pitched, impersonal voice was carefully declaiming the contents of the full-page article in *Il Tirreno*, one of the five the newspaper had given over to the murder in its local pages. Ampelio and Del Tacca were at the same table, listening intently without interrupting. Aldo was out shopping for his restaurant, as he was every morning. Massimo, with his usual concentration, was arranging the croissants, fresh from the oven, on the tray in the window. Every half-hour, Massimo would take five croissants at a time out of the oven and put them on the tray. If there were any left over from the previous batch, he would take them and put them in one of the little bags in which, in the course of the day, everything left over and no longer fit to serve ended up. That way everyone was happy: the customers, who could always count on warm croissants, Massimo, who charged an extra twenty cents on top of the price to guarantee this certainty, and the guests of the municipal dog pound who disposed of the rest, whether hot or cold. The croissants came from a bakery in Pisa, ready to be heated in the oven. Massimo had them delivered every morning, and they were one of the many details he considered essential.

"'The killer, having driven to the parking lot in the car belonging to the victim, a dark green Clio, license number CJ 063 CG, was unable to leave the parking lot because the vehicle was stuck in one of the large puddles that have been common after downpours for the past few years, in spite of the local authorities' repeated promises to take care of the problem. This was after depositing the body in one of the trashcans that—'"

"That are just like the ones I've had in front of the entrance of the restaurant for the last three months, damn those environmental organizations," Aldo said, entering laden with plastic bags.

"Here he is. Good health!"

"And prosperity! How are you all?"

He didn't get an answer, because just behind him, before the glass door had even closed, a princess had entered.

Or rather, a woman who looked every inch a princess. Tall, with short blond hair, wearing a dark blue tailored suit that must have cost a bomb, and gliding like a yacht, lightly and rhythmically, as if not even touching the floor. The last thing Massimo would have expected was that someone who walked like that would come up to the counter and lean her elbows on it, but that was exactly what she did.

"Good morning," she said.

She had a harsh, cold voice that jarred with the rest of her. Most likely she had slept badly.

"Good morning," Massimo replied. "What can I do for you?"

"You must be Massimo."

"That's correct. I'm the only thing in the bar that's not for sale. If you want one of those ornaments in the form of old men, you can have it. I recommend the one with the stick, it isn't very expensive."

"No, thanks," she said, without any change of expression. "Walter told me you're strange. I'm Arianna Costa. Alina's mother."

A few bursts of coughing from the old-timers greeted this statement. Massimo said nothing.

"He also told me you're a very serious person, and that you have a good brain."

"That's also correct."

The woman looked at him for a moment before speaking. "So if someone as serious and intelligent as you goes around saying that he knows the wrong person has been arrested for . . . for what happened to Alina, what does it mean?"

Massimo glared at the old-timers, who were pretending to mind their own business. "Exactly what you said."

"Why?"

"Because I'm reasonably certain of it. As to how I reached that certainty, now's not the time for me to tell you. I assure you I'll communicate it to those handling the investigation as soon as I can."

The woman slowly shook her head. "You know who it was, don't you? Either you know or you suspect."

"Not correct, this time. I don't have the slightest idea. All I can say is that whoever killed your daughter has certain characteristics that the young man we're talking about doesn't have."

"Are you pulling my leg?"

"Absolutely not. Would you like a drink?"

She looked at him for a moment, then nodded. "Is that Clément?"

"Yes, ten years old."

"Could I have a little?"

"Of course."

Massimo turned, took down the bottle of dark rum, poured a standard measure into a low glass, cut a small piece of melon, speared it with a toothpick, rolled it in cane sugar, and put it on a little saucer next to the glass. He felt it his duty to ask, "Isn't it a little early?"

"For you, maybe. For you it's morning. For me it's still night. I haven't slept for three days. I don't think I've quite realized yet what's happening."

"I understand."

"No, I don't think you do." She took a sip of the rum, and, in spite of what she had just said, coughed for a moment. "Are you really sure of what you told me about Bruno?"

"Yes, Signora."

Still looking at Massimo, the woman wet her lips in the glass. Finally she said, "In a way it's a relief. I can't bring myself to believe that Bruno's guilty. I wanted to come here after I overheard my maid talking about your theory. My husband didn't want me to, but I always do what I've made up my mind to do. I appreciate your frankness, and I'm grateful to you."

"Don't mention it. Is there anything I can do for you?"

"Speak to the inspector as soon as possible. Well, I'll leave you to your work. Goodbye."

"Goodbye."

And she went out with the same ethereal lightness with which she had entered.

"What a woman!" Pilade said.

"I agree," Aldo said. "And so calm. It's almost scary."

"Yes, scary," Massimo said, clearly and icily. "Almost as scary as the speed at which she managed to find out what I said last night."

"I didn't tell anyone," Ampelio said sulkily.

"Oh, you didn't tell anyone? Not even Grandma Tilde?"

"Yes, but your grandmother is family, if I can't tell her . . . "

"What about you, Pilade, did you tell your wife?"

"No, no, her sister Tilde told my wife, she phoned yesterday while she was at dinner." He looked at his watch. "Talking about eating, it's nearly lunch time. I'm going."

"Me too, I think," Rimediotti said.

"Not me," Aldo said, looking outside. "I don't want to miss the second round."

Massimo turned his head and also looked outside. Beyond the glass door, a few paces from the bar, he saw a very irritable Fusco advancing at a marching pace. Walking like that, Massimo thought, he looked even shorter.

"Hello. Coffee?" Massimo asked the inspector as soon as he had entered.

Fusco pretended not to hear him. He sat down at a table and started looking at him in silence, his head tilted slightly to one side, his black mustache completely hiding his lips. He's changed style, Massimo thought, now he's Poirot.

The old-timers were holding their breaths.

"Cappuccino? Fruit juice? *Créme de mènthe*? Sarsaparilla?" Massimo went on with apparent seriousness, meeting with the same silence. Only after a few seconds, spent still looking at Massimo with the expression of a man who has finally tracked down the person who made his daughter pregnant, did Fusco loosen up.

"As soon as you've stopped fucking with me," he said calmly, "I want you to come to the station. We need to talk."

"If the two of you want to talk here, it's no problem," Ampelio said magnanimously. "I swear we won't bother you!"

Massimo gave Ampelio a nasty look. Fusco continued looking at Massimo. That was a nasty look too.

"Investigations are usually conducted at police stations, not in bars. It seems to me there's been a bit of confusion on that point."

"Absolutely," Aldo interjected. "Investigations are indeed conducted at the station, but here the operations of the police are subject to the scrutiny of the community, because in a democratic country the citizen has a right to judge the police. He shouldn't merely accept things blindly, as I'm sure you—"

"Did anyone ask you?" Fusco cut in without turning to look at him.

Aldo fell silent, assuming a vaguely offended air.

"I need to talk to you at the station. If you don't mind abandoning the Greek chorus here for a few minutes I want you to come with me."

"Just a moment, I need to make a phone call."

"Hello?"

"Hi, Tiziana, Massimo here. Have you been awake for long?"

"Yes, I'm at the perfume store. I'm just paying."

"Perfect. As soon as you're out of there, can you drop by the bar for a moment?"

"Sure."

It was always a pleasure to see Tiziana, even though she wasn't at her best in the morning. As she approached the counter, Fusco, in spite of being on duty, gave her a head-to-foot X-ray, lingering briefly over her breasts, which were both soft and marmoreal.

"What is it?"

"Dr. Fusco here wants to take me to the station for a moment. Apparently it's urgent. I need you to mind the bar until I get back."

"'Can you drop by the bar for just a moment?'" Tiziana said, aping Massimo's clearly enunciated way of speaking. "God, what a liar you are. I have things to do."

"You can always refuse, it's your right. Let's see, I must still have the number of that girl in my diary, Loredana, if I remember correctly, the one who wanted to work here last summer. Let me see if I can find it. Oh, are you still here?"

"Massimo, I have more shopping to do . . . " Tiziana implored.

"This won't take long, Signorina, I can assure you," Fusco, who up until a moment earlier seemed to have been wondering if those were really nipples, said weakly. "And it is necessary."

"Can't Aldo stay behind the counter?"

"Negative, the youngsters are going to eat now. It's time. Oh, and another favor. Today's Wednesday, so the PR guys from the discos should be by to drop their vouchers. If the guys from the Ara Panic come while I'm away, can you tell them there's something I need to talk to them about?"

"Yes, bwana. Do you also have instructions about the cotton harvest?"

Massimo went back behind the counter, took his money pouch, and put his cigarettes and billfold in it.

"Send the old hospice here home for lunch, or my grandma will be at my throat. We can go now, Inspector."

"Let's go, then. Do you mind if we walk to the station?"

"In this heat, yes. But I don't see any other solution. After you."

SEVEN

Two hours later, at two-thirty, when Massimo got back, the bar was just about scraping a living in the sun-drenched post-lunch torpor. At the outside tables, tall Dutchmen and bespectacled Germans were mistreating their esophagi with daringly hot cappuccinos, all in the most religious silence, occasionally exchanging glaucous upward glances that probably meant: God, it's hot.

The Dutch, Massimo thought. In the old days, they must have been shut in, forbidden to cross the dikes on the border. But for some years now, wherever you turned you saw cars with yellow license plates, the six figures divided into two triplets, and with roof racks. (They all had to have roof racks— probably had to pay a heavy fine in cheese if they didn't.) So much for the economic recovery.

Inside, on the other hand, the natives were slowly beginning the process of peristalsis with a ritual that has always distinguished Italians in bars, one that can be performed any hour of the day or night at any establishment along the entire length of the Italian boot without running the risk that you will automatically be classified as a Kraut.

Espresso.

In the period under discussion, the Bar Lume offered ten different types of espresso, of which Massimo, as an Italian and a mathematician, was an enormous connoisseur not to say an obsessive: from a traditionally roasted Arabica supplied by a coffee store in Seravezza (this was what was served to anybody who simply asked for "an espresso"), to a Caracolito with small, fragrant beans, alas not always available, of which Massimo was as secretly proud as if he had made it himself.

He went behind the counter. "Everything okay?" he asked Tiziana.

"Yes everything's fine. How about you?"

"I'm fine. We have to make room for an ambulance out front."

"What?"

"An ambulance. For when one of those Visigoths swigging boiling hot cappuccinos at two-twenty in the afternoon gets such bad indigestion he bursts. If they keep going like that, it's bound to happen sooner or later."

"You're really obsessed, you know? You sound like my ma. This thing is bad for the digestion, that other thing swells your stomach, this one brings bad luck. Can't people do whatever they like?"

"In other bars, maybe. Here, no. Here, if someone asks for a cappuccino during the hottest part of the day, he needs to be told, politely but firmly, that much as we respect his daring, we can't allow him to do himself harm. If he's okay with that, fine. If he isn't, let him go to the Pennone for a cappuccino. That way, if he dies at least he'll die by the sea and he'll be happy."

"You're in a bad mood today," she said, emptying the ashtrays. "Fusco didn't listen to you, did he?"

Obviously, Ampelio had spilled the beans before he left.

"Of course not. Idiot."

"Can't you tell me why you think Messa had nothing to do with it?"

"No."

"Who do you think I'm going to tell? I'm no gossip. You should know that by now."

"Oh, yes," Massimo said in a slightly ironic tone. "I should know."

"Why do you say it like that?"

"How did I get to buy this bar?"

"What does that have to do with it?"

"Please answer me."

"You won the lottery."

"How many people here in Pineta know that?"

"I don't know . . . Everybody, I guess."

"Right. Seeing that, when I bought the bar, my grandfather, who might have been the prime suspect, was in hospital in Bellinzona because of his diabetic foot and my mother was there with him, and seeing that you were the only other person who knew about it, because I told you in a moment of distraction, is there something I should know?"

"God, you're really unbearable. I'll be back at six."

"You can come back at eight, you've been here two whole hours. Did the PR guys from the Ara Panic swing by?"

"Yes, they left the vouchers there next to the cash register."

"Tiziana, I don't give a damn about the vouchers. Did you tell them I wanted to talk to them?"

"I told them, I told them. They'll be back around six-thirty, seven. See you later."

"See you."

Soon afterwards, as Massimo was loading the dishwasher (which, being the moment in the day he hated the most, didn't help to improve his mood), Bruno's sister came into the bar. She was still dressed like Lolita, but seemed even more agitated than before.

"Hi."

"Hi."

"Is it true you went to the inspector to tell him that Bruno's innocent?"

"Yes, it is."

"Did he believe you?"

Massimo said nothing, but continued piling the glasses and dishes in the monster, taking care not to get his hands caught in the racks.

"Did he believe you?"

"No, I don't think so."

"Why don't you think so?"

"Because all I could tell him was a conclusion I've reached, and that's it. I don't have any evidence to give him."

"I'm sorry, I don't understand. How can you be sure it wasn't Bruno if you don't have evidence?"

"There was evidence, but it doesn't exist anymore. Something I noticed, but apparently nobody else thought anything of it. Fusco certainly doesn't."

"But he can't keep Bruno locked up! It wasn't him!"

"How do you know?"

The girl looked at him for a moment. She seemed really scared now. "I know him. He's my brother, after all."

"Precisely. That's not going to convince Fusco. Quite the opposite."

"I know it wasn't him. I talked to him."

"And he told you . . . "

"He told me where he was when Alina was killed. He was with other people."

Massimo looked at her, put the dishes down on his lap, and said, "That's perfect."

"Not really."

"All right, we know as much as before about who the murderer is, but at least your brother can get out of jail. Tell Fusco everything you know."

The girl shook her blond head. In spite of everything, she was impeccably made up, with a taste unusual in a girl her age. At least compared with those he knew or had known. She'd make a perfect housewife one day. It struck Massimo that there was no middle way in this nasty affair: they were either too rich, like Alina, like the doctor, like this girl, or too poor like O.K.

"He doesn't want to say anything."

"I get it. It's the people your brother knows. What was it, cocaine?"

The girl opened her eyes wide and stared at him, apparently without seeing him. "How do you know—"

"If you don't mind, I'm going to interrupt you there. Your brother's under arrest for murder, which would scare most people, and yet even though he has an alibi that would clear him he doesn't want to use it. That must mean there's something else he's even more scared of. And that something is what would happen if he talked, what would happen if the police found out where he was, what he was doing, who he was with. Whatever he was doing couldn't be worse than murder, so you don't have to be a rocket scientist to figure out he's scared of the people he was with. What did he do when Alina didn't show up? With people he's scared of? Correct me if I'm wrong, but I get the feeling it wasn't even the first time."

The girl did not reply. Massimo started piling the dishes again, and the girl turned and said, "I'm going."

"Have a nice day."

The door opened and closed.

Immediately afterwards the doctor's ironic voice rang out. "Excuse me, I'm looking for the Pineta police station. I've been told it's here."

"You've been wrongly informed," Massimo said, still arranging the dishes. "And you're not the only one."

Dr. Carli's face appeared over the counter like a giraffe at the zoo. He was smiling. "I know the girl who just went out. I wonder why she was here."

Silence.

"She has a brother who's in jail for murder."

Silence again.

"But I heard that this fellow who owns a bar is absolutely certain the brother is innocent. God knows why."

All right, then. The doctor sighed, still with the air of someone who doesn't take himself seriously, then, in a changed tone and a slightly louder voice, asked, "What do I have to do to rouse you?"

"Order something. As you so rightly said, this is a bar."

"And if I ask you for something will you give it to me?"

"Of course. If it's within my capabilities."

"Good. Then I'll have a cappuccino. With lots of chocolate on top. Was that a moan?"

"Yes, it was. Complete disapproval. Try again."

Having convinced the doctor that the most appropriate drink would be a fruit juice, they sat down at a table somewhere in the vicinity of Rotterdam. As soon as they were seated, the doctor said, "Massimo, don't take what I'm about to say in a bad way. I know, as we all do, that you're an extremely intelligent person and that you seldom talk without thinking. So even in this particular case, I'd like to believe you didn't say the first piece of nonsense that came into your head, but that you have a good reason for saying that a person who apparently has everything stacked against him, I don't mean evidence because it isn't, but anyway . . . Am I right?"

"I don't know. I haven't a clue what you're talking about. Try to put a period in there somewhere. Help me."

"What I'm trying to say is: Can you tell me why you're so sure of what you said?"

"Because you need periods to make the structure of the sentence clear to the person you're talking with. That's what I was taught at elementary school, and I'm sure of everything I was taught at elementary school."

"I don't think this is the right time to start playing the fool.

We're talking about a murder, and about a young man who may be innocent but is currently under arrest."

"Right. And I don't think this is the place to start talking about a murder, at least in terms of the investigation. This is a bar. I've tried to take everything back to its natural place, in other words, the police station, but your immediate superior wouldn't even give me a second glance."

The doctor frowned. "In other words, you went to see Fusco and he didn't believe you?"

"Precisely."

For a moment, the doctor weighed up the situation in silence. Then he made himself more comfortable on his chair and said, "Listen, there is something we can do. The only thing I can think of."

"Go on."

"Fusco thinks you're a pain in the neck, that I know for sure. Just as I know for sure that someone as pig-headed as he is won't reopen a case when he has a perfectly acceptable culprit just because a barman says the fellow is innocent. But he has a certain amount of respect for me, at least on a professional level. So here's what I suggest we do. You explain to me clearly why you're so sure the boy isn't guilty, and I go see Fusco and do everything I can to persuade him to reopen the case. Is that O.K. with you?"

"Yes, I don't think there's anything else we can do."

"Then tell me your deductions."

"I don't have any deductions, just an observation. One you may even have made yourself."

The doctor gave a little smile. "I see. That's better still, isn't it? Go on."

"The morning the body was found, Fusco made a fool of himself in a lot of ways, do you remember?"

"Of course. When that young man said his car was a Micra—"

"Then," Massimo interrupted him, "you remember Fusco had the wrong car moved. And do you remember who he asked to move it?"

"Yes, Pardini. His father and I were at elementary school together. But I'm sorry, how does that—"

He was about to say "fit in," but Massimo interrupted him again. "So Fusco tells Officer Pardini to move the car. Follow me, this is important. Do you remember what Pardini did?"

"Yes, he went to the car and moved it."

"By lifting it?"

"No. You love splitting hairs, don't you? He got in the car, sat down, turned the key, put his foot on the accelerator, and the car moved. Did I pass?"

"No, you failed miserably. You forgot the most important thing, which is that Pardini adjusted the seat. He adjusted the seat by moving it forward. I'm sure, because I remember that it struck me at the time. It struck me that whoever had been driving that car before must have been very tall, seeing that Pardini's about six feet. So when I heard that Bruno Messa, who apart from all his other faults is almost a midget, had been arrested I thought they must have the wrong person."

The doctor looked at him. He seemed impressed, but not convinced, and his first words confirmed this. "That doesn't seem like much to me."

"But on top of that, I know what Bruno Messa was doing during the time when he's supposed to have killed Alina. As soon as he's gotten over the fear of being caught with his pants down, I hope he'll confide in someone the way his sister did with me. It's better to get a suspended sentence for buying cocaine than spend thirty years picking up bars of soap in the shower that have been dropped by guys a lot bigger and nastier than you."

"Uh-huh. And his sister told you this?"

"That's right. He's afraid to admit it right now, but sooner or later he'll see reason."

"Remarkable. But she only just told you?"

"Yes."

"That means you were already sure, based on what you remembered, that—"

"Precisely."

"Then let me ask you a question, even though I know it'll make you mad. The murderer must be very tall, he must be . . . "

"He must be tall. He must be someone who knew Alina, even if now he tries to deny it. He must be someone who doesn't have an alibi for the two hours between eleven and one when Alina was killed."

"Okay. And do you have any ideas?"

Just then, Tiziana arrived.

"Massimo, the PR guys from the Ara Panic are back. They're waiting for you inside, as soon as you can."

EIGHT

ere we are, Massimo told himself. Now what am I going to ask these two? Excuse me, you know P.G., the bouncer at the disco where you work? Yes? Do you know if by any chance he killed a girl on Saturday night? My God, how muscular they are. Obviously, they work out. Nothing special about that. Thousands and thousands of push-ups and the biceps are bound to swell, but it's all a fake. Pectorals like potato starch, if you punched them they'd shift to the back and look like humps. Okay, but right now they're the ones with the great physiques, and you've been meaning to join a gym for the past two years, haven't you? Except that it's too hot now, then in the fall the championship matches start again, in January I have to fast for a month to recover from Christmas, and you still want me to go to the gym? You want me to kick the bucket just so we don't have to talk about it again? February is a month that doesn't count, March is the beginning of spring and I don't feel like doing anything at all, and then it's summer again and you look the same as you did, with a physique like a coat hanger. And anyway, you studied so much . . .

"Hi."

"Hi. I'm Massimo."

"Dennis. This is Davide," the young man said, indicating a photocopy of himself, who nodded. Slightly curly hair shaped with gel, wide single-lens sunglasses in light frames shaped like a minimalist scrotum, shirts with sleeves rolled up, open on shaved chests.

"Would you like a drink?"

The two said no in unison.

"I wanted to ask you if you could give me some gen about the timetable of the disco, when things start, when they finish, and so on."

"Some gen? You mean . . . "

"Some information. What time you open, what time people start arriving, what time you close. Let me explain . . . "

Here Massimo had planned to say how he had noticed that in the big towns along the coast it had become fashionable for groups of young people to round off the night by all going to have breakfast in a bar after the disco. Knowing that those who left the discos in Pineta—the Imperiale, the Negresses and the Ara Panic—either went to Pisa for breakfast or didn't go anywhere at all because there weren't any bars already open and functioning at that hour in Pineta or the surrounding area, he wanted to organize things so that his bar was ready to welcome and feed the thousands of young people emerging deafened from the local discos. There was no need to say any of that crap, though, because Dennis—or Davide?—in the true spirit of public relations, launched straight in:

"Well, the club gets going at around midnight, in the sense that the DJs start to turn up the music and the go-go dancers warm up a bit. In the meantime the lines form, although people don't actually come in until one. We're partly inside, partly outside, giving out cards for the themed nights if there are any planned, stuff like that. The DJs stop at four, and people leave between four and four-thirty."

"Why does it take so long?"

The two men looked at each other, then Davide (maybe) cottoned on. "To pay, right? People pay when they leave.

That's how it works, admission plus one obligatory drink comes to twenty-five. When you go in you don't pay anything, when you get a drink they give you a card with what you drank written on it and on your way out you go to the cashier and pay. There are three cashiers, but it still takes time. On special dates there are more than five hundred people. The average is about three hundred."

"I'm sorry, what do you mean by special dates? Themed nights with particular music . . . "

"That's right. We do 80s nights, for example, hip hop nights, funk nights. Or else there are guests, this year we had the people from *Big Brother*, the cast of the soap opera *A Place in the Sun*, right now we're in touch with Valentino Rossi the motorcycle racer, he's supposed to be coming at the end of the summer but he's a bit tied up because he has so many different fan clubs. Roberto Farnesi the actor came last week, the night that girl was murdered. God, that was a busy night . . . "

"You should be used to it."

"Yes, but when there are soap stars there's always a whole lot of screaming girls outside, they don't come in, they just wait outside for three hours, and we have to hold them off because if something happens the club gets in trouble. Plus, we were on our own that night because Renzo wasn't there, P.G. arrived late, there were three of us against fifty. Every now and then the father of one of the girls would show up, give her a slap and drag her away, and we'd shout and say 'Please, Signore, calm down,' but actually we were grateful because that meant one more off our hands. Some of these girls . . . "

What a cross, kid! Massimo thought. Perfectly centered, clean, precise. One little tap and it's a goal.

"Yes, I can imagine," he said, the image of affability now. "Just the three of you with all that commotion going on? You probably had to hold out for about an hour . . . "

"An hour?" D. bristled. "Two and a half hours we were

there! From midnight until two-thirty. That idiot P.G. showed up after everyone else and actually got down to work, but shit, he should have been there earlier. And he even flew off the handle when we told him, he started yelling that he'd been inside all the time, and I said to him, 'Then you're an asshole, you leave us alone with all this commotion? You've got shit for brains.' He hadn't even been inside, you know. He'd been fucking someone for sure. And that wasn't the first time. Sorry if I get upset but that's the way it is, and then we always get the blame . . . "

"No, I understand. Anyway, what I get from all this is, if a bar is open from four o'clock, people will come, right?"

There was a brief silence. The other guy, who hadn't yet opened his mouth, thought it over for a moment, then made up his mind. "You're talking about your bar, right? Look, I don't know. I get what you want to do, it may not be such a bad idea, but you know what the problem is? You're too close. When people leave, they usually get in their cars and go to Pisa or Livorno to meet up with friends who've been to other places. You're a little bit out of the way here, in my opinion. Now I may be wrong. But anyway, that's what I think . . . "

"You could be right. Anyway I just wanted to get an idea. I don't know much about discos, that's why . . . Thanks for dropping by."

"Do you need anything else? If you do, anything at all, here's the number."

Public relations, of course. Nice to meet you, anyway. You could always come in useful. Massimo took the card the guy was holding out to him and put it in his billfold, and as he did so noticed that his hands were shaking. Talking bullshit always made him nervous.

Massimo went back outside and rejoined the doctor, who had been waiting for him. As soon as he sat down, the doctor said, "Listen, I'm going to see Fusco and tell him what we said before. I hope I can get him to change his mind, though I don't know how likely that is. Before I do, I have to ask you again if, in all honesty, you're absolutely sure of what you told me. Sorry if I insist, but you realize I have a personal interest in this matter."

"Yes, I'm sure."

Dr. Carli stood up, carefully draped his light jacket over his forearm and put his chair back in its place. "In that case, I'm off," he said. "I'll be back as soon as I've talked with Fusco."

"If you're planning to go see Fusco right now, it's best if you sit down again."

"Why?"

"Because there's something important I have to tell you."

"Will it take long?"

"Fairly."

The doctor put his jacket on the back of the chair and sat down, resigned.

The doctor sat quite still while Massimo told him what the guys from the Ara Panic had said. By the end, he seemed vaguely disconcerted.

"So, let's sum up the situation for a moment, if you don't mind. Bruno Messa can't be guilty because (a)"—he took hold of his thumb—"he's too short and (b)"—his index finger—"because he was somewhere else when the murder took place. Correct?"

"Correct."

"So"—the doctor squeezed his middle finger—"the murderer must be someone very tall, who knew Alina and doesn't have an alibi for the hours between midnight and one, the time of the murder. Correct?"

"Almost. He also doesn't have an alibi for the hour between four-thirty and five-thirty, when the body was found. But obviously he must have been doing something between the time of the murder and the time he hid the body four or five hours later. The inspector told you that O.K. saw the trash can was empty at about four-thirty, didn't he?"

"Yes, he did." The doctor looked at Massimo for a few moments, then smiled and gave a kind of half-bow with his head. "You've been lucky, you know . . . "

Massimo nodded slowly, also smiling with his eyes. There were a few moments of silence, which the doctor then broke.

"So it seems we've found him."

It wasn't a question.

"I'm not sure yet, I have no motive and no proof." Massimo stood up and put his chair back under the table. "But frankly . . . "

"I'm going to see Fusco, then."

"Have a nice day."

Inside the bar, Massimo found the happy gang of pensioners, apart from Aldo, arrayed in front of the TV and laughing like drains as a heavily made-up (but male) fortune teller said in a shrill, whiny voice, "Don't you get it? Look, darling, the cards are quite clear and I'm sorry to have to say this, but he really doesn't want you anywhere near him, you know? Look, I wouldn't waste any more time on him, I tell you that right now, you know? The cards are very clear, my darling. Just look . . . What? So what? Find yourself another man! I'm a fortune teller, I'm not your mother! I tell it the way it is! If you like it, fine, if you don't like it, too bad. It's clear from the cards that he wouldn't touch you with a ten-foot pole, all right? Producer, can you cut off this caller please? Oooooh! The things I have to listen to! 'What should I do, Ofelio? What should I do?' I'll tell you what to do! Wake up! You're ugly, all right, I got that. There's a remedy for everything. Buy yourself a nice barrel, stick a periscope in it, and go for a walk! But if you keep breaking everyone's balls like this, you're never going to find a man, right, girl? Not even a duck-billed platypus would go for someone like you. I apologize to the people at home but hey, every now and again you have to let it all hang out."

Ampelio let out a loud laugh. "I can imagine how you let it all hang out!"

Pilade now joined in. "God, what a queer!"

"What about you, Rimediotti, don't you have anything to add?" Massimo asked icily.

"Oh, come on, Massimo, don't take it like that!"

"I know how that fellow there takes it," Ampelio said in a low voice, pointing at the TV.

"Obviously I haven't made myself clear. You're in a bar, not in your own homes. There's the possibility that some people might not like you. Including me, of course. And since it happens that this place is mine, the fact of not liking you might be of some consequence."

Ampelio calmed down, muttering between his teeth something like "Narrow minded . . . " and Massimo again started loading the dishwasher. As he leaned over the monster, he heard someone come in. Immediately, Aldo's cheerful voice rang out.

"Hello everyone, ugly and handsome alike. What are you watching on TV?"

"An astrology show," Pilade said without taking his eyes off the screen.

"Cool," Aldo said, turning to look at the TV.

"Just think, in my days they called it taking it in the ass, now they call it astrology."

"Ah, the things you learn from TV . . . " Pilade said smugly.

NINE

D rriiiiiing.
Drriiiiiing.
Drriiiiiing.
"Hello?"

"Hello, it's Aldo."

"Hello."

"Hello, Massimo, it's Aldo. I wanted to—"

"Hello? I can't hear a thing."

"Massimo, it's Aldo," Aldo said a little louder.

"Speak louder. I can hardly hear a thing."

"Mas-si-mo" Aldo yelled, emphasizing each syllable, "they called me from the pol-ice sta-tion. They want—"

"There's no point shouting like that," Massimo said calmly. "This is a recording. Leave a message after the beep."

"Fuck off," Aldo said after a brief moment of consternation.

"Bar Lume, hello."

"Hello, Tiziana? Massimo here. Is Aldo there?"

"Massimo, things are chaotic here. Fusco called you a dozen times, then came here in person and almost arrested your grandpa. I'll pass him to you, he's here."

"Thanks."

"Signor Viviani?"

"Speaking."

"I need you to come to the station as soon as you can."

"Of course. Why did you try to arrest my grandfather? Not that I'm complaining . . . "

"We can speak at the station. See you later."

Better get dressed. God, Massimo told himself, if the man isn't breaking balls he's not happy.

Massimo walked into the station to find the doctor sitting on one of the chairs and Fusco with his buttocks propped on the window sill. Both responded to his greeting with a grunt, the doctor's cordial and the inspector's somewhat pig-like.

"Please sit down."

"Hello, Massimo." The doctor got out of the chair and walked to the other window.

"We called you because there have been some new developments," the inspector said. "We realize you've been a great help. Thanks to you, we've avoided making an over-hasty accusation. Obviously, you can't have any official role in our investigation. But . . . "

"But?"

"The fact is . . . well, people seem to trust you. You managed to get hold of information about the case we knew nothing about it. In short . . . "

Embarrassing, isn't it? Poor thing, I know how you must feel, Massimo thought smugly.

The doctor took over, in a contemptuous tone. "Messa has confessed where he was when the murder took place. Apparently the boy, who obviously has more money than sense, is in the habit of clearing his nose with a medication that isn't on the list of officially approved drugs. That's why, when he needs to fire up that negligible lump of guano he has instead of a brain, he meets with his friends in a dark place and buys a little cocaine. Which is what he says he did on the night in question."

"He's also told us who sold it to him," the inspector cut in. "A small-time dealer we've known about for a while now. It won't be hard to confirm this alibi, although I fear it may take some time. So it's our opinion that the young man should be released, although personally, with all the time he's made us waste, I'd happily squeeze his fingers in a vise, but that too"— the inspector raised his eyes to heaven—"is an opinion. However, I'm convinced there are still some things he hasn't told us, and so for the moment he needs to remain available. Right now, there's another matter to discuss. The thing is . . . "

"The thing is, Massimo," the doctor took over, giving Massimo a meaningful stare, "I've told the inspector what you found out from the PR guys at the disco, and we both realize that the finger now points rather firmly at Piergiorgio Neri, known as P.G. In addition . . . "—the doctor glanced at the inspector, who encouraged him with a look to continue—"in addition, it emerged from the post mortem that the girl was pregnant. A few weeks pregnant."

Silence. That too? Well, given the life she led, and all the men who had her, it was hardly surprising. If the poor girl was an easy lay, that was the kind of thing that could happen. The problems arise when you convince yourself it can only happen to other people . . .

The significance of the doctor's statement only became evident a moment later, stemming the tide of nonsense in Massimo's brain.

"Do you know who the father was?" he asked.

The inspector showed off his specialty, in other words he glared at him, then allowed himself a brief smile. "We have the genetic imprint of the fetus, of course. But to establish who the father is we'd have to make comparisons, and in order to make comparisons we need samples." He paused, put his hands together, and started opening and closing his fingers like a whiskery little seal. "Samples of material that would be admissible as evidence in a court of law. I can hardly disguise myself as a gypsy woman, stop people on the street, and pull out hairs to protect them against the evil eye. Especially as the list of candidates seems to be a long one . . . " Here the doctor glared at Fusco, who hastened to change the subject. "Anyway, I think we understand each other. If you let me have a statement about what you saw when we found the body and about the conversation you had with those two young men, and also tell me their names, I can summon Neri" (Neri? Massimo thought. Oh, yes, P.G.) "as a witness. If I don't like his answers, and I don't see how I could like them given that he keeps denying he ever knew the girl, I'll detain him as a suspect and ask for his DNA to be compared with that of the fetus. If they're identical, then God help him, I'll get him sooner or later." The inspector drummed with his fingers on the window sill, then said to Massimo, "Well?"

"Well, of course, I'm happy to do that. The two PR guys are called Dennis and Davide, they shouldn't be hard to find. As for the statement, here I am."

"Perfect. You could even make it right now, if the doctor doesn't mind leaving. I'll type it personally."

The doctor intercepted Massimo's questioning look. "Officer Pardini somehow managed to break his wrist falling off his chair, and Officer Tonfoni has gone with him to the Santa Chiara hospital in Pisa to have it treated. Why are you smiling?"

"Oh, no reason, just the way I am. All right, let's start."

" ' . . . As the vehicle was being removed from the location where it had been discovered, I noticed that the driver's seat was positioned quite far back, so as to render driving impossible for anyone other than those of above average height, to such an extent that even the officer charged with the removal, Enrico Pardini (whose is about six feet tall) found himself obliged to move the said seat forward in such a way as to allow himself to maneuver the vehicle easily. Being . . . ' Blah, blah, blah. OK, that seems fine," Fusco said.

"Of course," Massimo said, admiring Fusco's ability to translate his plain, linear statement into that magnificent baroque tangle that satisfied all the age-old canons of legal language. Obviously, Fusco, with the speed and dexterity of a champion skier, had skirted any trace of the things he'd done to make a fool of himself on the morning in question, but what mattered was that what Massimo had seen was now down in black and white.

"Good, now just read and sign."

Massimo read it, nodded approvingly, as he did when he didn't understand a damned thing or when he wasn't paying much attention to what he was reading or listening to, and signed with the signature he had learned in elementary school, the signature he hated so much, with the M made up of three perfect little arches looking down on the remaining letters, all written with pedantic precision and all clearly distinguishable.

"We may still need you, so please remain available. Can you give me your cell phone number?"

"No."

"I'm sorry?"

"I don't have a cell phone. If you don't find me at home you'll find me in the bar. If I'm not in either of those two places, I'll be there some time during the day. And there's always someone in the bar."

"All right, I've made a note of that. And tell your grandfather to be less of a smart ass, or the next time I really will arrest him."

When Massimo got back to the bar, he was greeted by a cheerful ovation from the old-timers.

"Three cheers for Sherlock Holmes!"

"So how did it go? Did you pass?"

"I did, yes. So did Aldo. Someone else didn't do so well. Isn't that so, grandpa?"

Ampelio smiled. "What's it got to do with me?"

"What did you tell Fusco?"

"I told him what he deserved to hear. I said, 'Have you been transferred to the traffic police, because I'm always seeing you here in the bar instead of where you ought to be?'"

Massimo laughed. "You're really something. How about a game of *briscola*? I have to go out again later."

Chairs under the table, a glass to mark the place, and away we go. We're not here for anybody. I did my duty, Massimo told himself, now it's up to those who get paid for it. From now on, I'm just a barman again.

A nyway, what I wanted to say to you is simply that this business may ruin my client completely. And when I say completely, I mean completely. Both as a professional and as a man. I don't think there's any need to explain why. Nobody would trust him, after . . . after what's happened."

Understandably, Massimo thought. Right now, he was starting to wonder why he had accepted an invitation from P.G.'s lawyer to have dinner at the Boccaccio.

It wasn't that he hadn't expected to hear from P.G., mind you. After all that had happened, the absence of any reaction from the man himself would have implied:

(a) that P.G. did not know that Massimo had played a major role in orienting the investigation, and therefore in screwing things up for him, or:

(b) that P.G. intended simply to stay calm, think things through, and await further developments.

The fact that they were both in Pineta made possibility (a) simply unthinkable, and even a slight knowledge of the person in question *de facto* ruled out possibility (b).

So Massimo had expected to hear from P.G., one way or another. From what he knew of the guy, however, he would have expected him to come into the bar, the veins of his neck artfully swollen, with a couple of eager helpers pretending to hold him back while he tried to beat Massimo up, or something like that. With Fusco's arrest of P.G., however, this eventuality had become highly unlikely, and so Massimo had stopped expecting any direct reaction on the part of P.G.

But there had in fact been a reaction from P.G..

It was about three-thirty the previous day, and the bar was blissfully enjoying a well-deserved post-prandial rest. Massimo was sitting behind the counter with his feet soaking in a tub filled with water, reading *The Remains of the Day* by Kazuo Ishiguro (a great book, but one to be read when you're in a good mood, or you're likely to throw yourself under a streetcar). The senate was outside in the shade of the big lime tree, playing canasta and so not kicking up the usual fuss, for once in a while. A not very tall man, with round metal-rimmed glasses and a touch of hair at the sides and in the middle of a shiny cranium, got out of a Z4, entered the bar with a smile on his face, and greeted Massimo in a loud voice, "Good afternoon."

"It depends."

"I'm sorry?"

"It depends on your intentions. If you simply want to have a cold drink and enjoy the shade outside, I could continue to read peacefully for a while longer and therefore it would continue to be a good afternoon at least for the time being. If on the other hand it's your intention to talk about the Costa murder, that would force me to close my book, which would fall into the category of things that piss me off. If that were the case, your greeting would strike me as patently hypocritical."

(In Massimo's defense, it should be said that when he was reading a good book he tended to empathize strongly with the author and his way of writing, and that the book in question is narrated in the first person by an English butler at the end of the Second World War. Leaving aside the concept of something pissing you off, which was somewhat alien to the way a top-grade manservant would express himself, it can't be ruled out that Massimo's reply was heavily influenced by the language that Ishiguro attributes to Stevens the butler).

In the moment of embarrassment that followed, the only sounds were the rustle of a page being turned and, from outside, a weak, apparently senile voice saying to hell with you and your stupid canasta, you idiot, if you used your brain at least once a year it'd do you a lot of good.

Still smiling, the man said, "What makes you think I want to talk about the Costa murder?"

"Because only yesterday I saw a photograph of you in *Il Tirreno*, and underneath it there was a caption saying 'Attorney Luigi Nicola Valenti, Piergiorgio Neri's defense lawyer,'" Massimo said without taking his eyes off the book. "Right now, Piergiorgio Neri known as P.G. is suspected of the murder of Alina Costa, on the basis of evidence I helped to supply. Given that even in this era when all the rules tend to be broken, two plus two stubbornly continues to make four, it struck me as obvious that you wanted to talk about something that concerns your client."

The smile never once leaving his face, Attorney Valenti jumped up onto one of the stools at the counter. "They told me you were very observant, and they were right. They also told me you're decidedly unfriendly."

"Wrong," Massimo said, continuing to read. "I'm actually very friendly. I simply hate it when people feel they have the right to piss me off, and ever since that girl was murdered, that's something that's been happening rather a lot. Would you like a drink?"

"Why not? Could I have a coffee?"

"No, it's out of reach."

"I'm sorry?"

"As you can see, right now my movements are somewhat restricted because my feet are in a tub. The coffee machine is too far. You can have everything you see at this end of the counter—iced tea, beer, water and cold drinks, Sicilian granita made the way it should be, either with genuine lemons from Erice or with coffee. That's quite a choice, I'm sure you'll agree."

"Er . . . a granita with coffee, please."

"With cream or without?

"Without, thanks. So—"

"With brioche or without?"

"Granita with brioche? This is the first I've heard of that."

"Really?" Massimo seemed genuinely upset. "How disappointing. Well?"

"Without, thanks," Attorney Valenti said, starting to betray a modicum of irritation.

Massimo stood up with his feet still in the water, put a cardboard coaster as a bookmark in the page he had reached, and put the book down. There was no sound anywhere, either inside or out.

"So," the lawyer said. "At this point it seems to me that the best thing to do is not waste too much time, but tell you why I'm here. In a nutshell, my client has asked me to meet with you."

"In what sense?" Massimo asked, as usual playing mentally with the image of a scoreboard announcing "Tonight, major bout for the regional heavyweight and welterweight titles between the champion Piergiorgio Neri, known as P.G., and the loser Massimo Viviani, known as the Barman," and beneath it photographs of both the contenders in dressing gowns.

"In the sense that two civilized people—you and I, in this case—sit down at a table and talk, in order to understand what has happened and decide on the best strategy to adopt."

"I don't get it. Why do we need a strategy?"

"To see to it that the truth emerges. To make sure that the

heap of coincidences and false assumptions that have somehow been twisted into indications of my client's guilt is untan-
gled. You must be aware that—"

"All I'm aware of is that I really ought to change the sign
outside. I have to take away the one that says *Bar* and put up a
marble one saying *Police Station*"—here Massimo began to
raise his voice—"so that at last people will again start coming
in here and asking for a coffee, instead of breaking my balls
about the murder! The next time I find a body in a trash can,
I'll go to the police and accuse myself of the murder, dammit!
At least that way I might get some peace and quiet for a while."

"All right, but you must agree that—"

"No, *you've* obviously all agreed to come here one at a time,
first to make me find a body, then to make me find a murderer,
and now even to free him. Hello, Tiziana," he said to the girl,
who had just come in. "Quite frankly, I'm finding it all too
much."

Attorney Valenti did not speak for a moment. He took a
spoonful of granita, put it in his mouth, and seemed to like the
taste. Then, looking down at the granita, he said, "Will you
allow me to say something?"

"Go ahead. It's a free country."

"Precisely. It's a free country. A country where we all have
rights. That implies that we also have duties, and it's thanks to
our respecting those duties, in principle anyway, that we're
able to maintain our rights. Have I been clear so far?"

"Yes."

"Good. In life things are the way they are, not the way we'd
like them to be. I'm sorry you've been dragged into a murder
case that seems to have nothing to do with you, and that you've
then been pulled even further into it because of some things
you observed and because you know some people connected
with it. We agree, you have no intention of continuing to be
involved. However, by an unfortunate chance, you know

things about the case, you're a witness. It's not so much that you're involved, it's that you have a duty to be involved. It just happened to you, all right, but allow me to point out that there are people in this case that far worse things have happened to. So stop playing the victim and do your duty, after which you can go back to your book. Unless, as you were hoping earlier, someone arrests you first and mistakenly accuses you of the murder. That seems to be happening a lot around here lately."

The attorney took a business card from his pocket and held it out to Massimo. Massimo took it, looked at it and said, "Tell me when."

"Dinner tomorrow?"

"All right. I'll call to arrange it. Goodbye."

As the lawyer was going out, Massimo, simulating feigned indifference, asked in a loud voice, "Tiziana, can you fill in for me at dinner time tomorrow?"

"Of course, boss. Anything to allow you to carry out your duty."

"Thanks."

"Nice man, that lawyer, wasn't he?"

"We were just talking about my duties. You want me to remind you what yours are, or were you planning to clean the toilet anyway?"

Tiziana came out from behind the counter with the bucket and the gloves, and stuck her tongue out at Massimo. "You're spiteful, you know."

Massimo picked up his book and ostentatiously removed the coaster. "I hate being wrong," he said in a low voice.

"Wow. That's the first time I've heard you admit it."

"It's the first time you've been here when it happened. Don't say anything to the old-timers or I'll strangle you."

And so Massimo, fully living up to his new role as a Serious Person, had found himself having dinner with the lawyer. They had sat down at a slightly isolated table in the so-called artists' room at the Boccaccio.

The artists' room at the Boccaccio was so called because there were a few posters by Aldo's favorite painters, Hokusai and Jack Vettriano, on the walls, unlike the other rooms, which displayed bloodcurdling daguerreotypes of sailors and field hands from the previous century alternating with big blow-ups of the cook photographed in his hunting jacket with the most beautiful catches of his career.

Massimo and the lawyer talked about this and that over dinner. In spite of his law degree, Attorney Valenti was quite an intelligent, widely read man, although not an especially witty one. It was not until after coffee that he revealed his anxieties, in the manner already quoted.

"There's one thing I don't understand," Massimo said.

"What's that?"

"P.G., I mean your client, has been arrested. That's all. What I don't understand is why you're so worried. Are you sure that, as things stand, he'd be found guilty?"

"No, not at all. There's no evidence. There's no motive. There's only the testimony of a barman—I'm sorry, but that's the way it is—who says that the seat of the victim's car had been moved a long way back. Admittedly, there's my client's lack of an alibi. But in any trial worthy of the name, we wouldn't even get to the alibi. We're not in Burundi. Here, in order for a man to be found guilty of murder, his guilt must be demonstrated beyond a reasonable doubt. If there's no evidence and there's no motive, no jury would find him guilty. Even arresting him was an exaggeration, though you can't expect anything better from someone like our inspector."

"Well, then?" Massimo asked.

"The problem is that although, from the point of view of the State, my client can't be found guilty, the community found him guilty quite some time ago. Let me put it more clearly. My client knows that this is a small town."

"And people whisper," Massimo said automatically.

"Congratulations! People whisper. The local papers write, and they write what the people want to hear. We have papers that talk almost exclusively about disasters, and that aren't objective even when they talk about the weather, so they're hardly going to be held back by ethics when it comes to a case like this. People read the papers, comment on them, and come to conclusions. My client will become 'the man who killed the girl and got away with it.' He wants to avoid all that."

Then he has to kill the rest of the town, Massimo would have liked to say. Instead, he decided to continue playing the Serious Person and limited himself to asking, "What's he planning to do?"

"According to him, there's only one way out. And I agree with him. Find the culprit, and prove his guilt."

"Then I'll repeat the question. What's he planning to do?"

"We have to reconstruct everything from the beginning. Question the victim's friends, reconstruct her last day. Discover where she was during that period of time when nobody saw her. Dig deep. There's no magic formula, unfortunately."

"I'm sorry, but what this got to do with me?"

"You were at the scene when the body was found, but as far as that's concerned"—the lawyer smiled—"you've already made your contribution. But I know you're friendly with the victim's best friend. I mean Giada Messa, the first suspect's sister."

"Not exactly. I know her."

"All right, you know her. How would you feel about exploiting that acquaintanceship?"

"That depends," Massimo said, imagining various meanings of the word "exploitation" with a seventeen-year-old Lolita as protagonist.

"How would you feel about discreetly asking this girl and her brother specific questions about the victim? Questions I'd suggest to you?"

"I don't know. I don't think I'm the right person to do that."

"Nonsense. I'm sorry, but in cases like this, people are more likely to confide in a stranger than in their friends, or the police. I don't think the girl told the police everything she knows, especially after they arrested her brother. Apart from anything else, you got her brother out of jail. Because of that, I think they'll both trust you. The brother might also have some useful information. After all, he and the victim were supposed to meet on the night of the murder. It's possible he too hasn't revealed everything he knows. You would be very useful in that respect."

Massimo felt ill at ease. On the one hand, he was curious to know how things were going to end up. On the other, the thought of getting involved in this nasty business again made him feel bad.

"I'm sorry, but I have to be frank with you. I don't think this would get us anywhere. We each believe what we believe, whether we're right or wrong. But I'm not inclined to question people. Irritate them, yes. Make them think sometimes. But getting them to talk, being understanding when they tell me their life stories, no. I have a problem with that. I don't feel up to it."

"I understand, but you have to understand me. It's the only chance we have to reopen the investigation."

At this point, an explanation is in order. At a conservative estimate, there were about ten thousand situations potentially capable of irritating Massimo. But if there was one thing that irritated Massimo more than anything else, it was saying no to somebody and then the other person not giving a damn and keeping right on trying to persuade him as if he were a six-year-old. This applied to everyone, from street vendors to his own mother. Whenever it happened, Massimo invariably lost his temper.

"Obviously, I haven't made myself clear. I don't want to do it. And I don't want to do it because I'm not suited to what you're asking of me. I'm telling you this for the last time because I have no intention of changing my mind. Please don't insist."

"Don't worry. We'll sort it out together. We just have to—"

"Goodbye."

And he got up and walked out. Leaving the other man to pick up the tab, of course. But as the man was a lawyer, there shouldn't have been any problem about that.

Later, at home and already in bed, Massimo continued to reflect on the evening. On one thing, in particular, that he had told the lawyer. The lawyer had asked him to ask questions. To ask questions *discreetly.* That didn't make any sense to Massimo. If he wanted to make sure the case was reopened, why act discreetly? Why not make waves? Because, Massimo answered himself, it wasn't in his interests to make waves. *Ergo*, he really might be interested in doing what he had said: finding out who the real murderer was.

Massimo had taken it for granted that the lawyer was working only in the interests of his client, which was why he had lost his temper and left like a child who doesn't want to play ball anymore. Now he was no longer so sure.

On the other hand, there was one thing he was very sure of.

That the murder had come back into his head, and wasn't going to leave any time soon.

TEN

"'Too Many Question Marks, Bouncer Remains in Gail by Pericle Bartolini.

"Let's have some quiet, shall we?

"'Pineta: After four hours of questioning, the position of Piergiorgio Neri, popularly known as P.G., for some time now a lively figure on the disco scene in Pineta, has become clearer, and he is now officially under investigation. Questioned yesterday by Deputy Prosecutor Artemio Fioretto, the bouncer reconstructed his movements on the day of the murder, assisted by his lawyer, Luigi Nicola Valenti.'—Must be the son of Valenti from San Piero, who used to repair bicycles.—'The version of events supplied by Neri is simple: he claims that after coming back from a boat trip with some friends he was at home from eight in the evening until one in the morning, suffering from acute stomach pains and high fever, caused by eating rotten food.'—And I suppose it was too much of an effort to lift the phone, that's why he didn't call anyone. Do me a favor!—'Since nobody has come forward to confirm this, and the deputy prosecutor himself has ordered that Neri remain in custody'—seems to me that's the least they can do—'at least until the DNA test, planned for today, thanks to which the police should know if the fetus was biologically the child of Neri himself, and be able to establish a possible connection between him and the victim. A connection that has so far eluded them, in spite of their obvious belief that the bouncer knows much more about the murder that he is prepared to say. There are in fact too many things linking Neri and the description of the murderer: not having an alibi either for the period between eleven and one, when the girl was killed, or for the period between four-thirty and six the following morning, when the body was hidden in the trash can. In addition, Neri is six and a half feet tall, which tallies with the fact that, according to the findings of the forensics team,'—if you waited for them, you could wait forever—'the driver of the vehicle in which the girl was transported to that her terrible, improvised coffin must have been unusually tall.'

Like you, Pilade." Ampelio lowered the newspaper and took a tiny sip of his hated iced tea.

Del Tacca, who had been exempted from military service because he was just over five feet tall, had finished his ice cream and was getting ready to light his dreaded unfiltered Stop. "Listen to me, dammit," he said, putting the cheap cigarette in his mouth, "firstly the reason I'm short is because my brain has been weighing me down all my life, secondly if you don't stop making stupid comments, we'll wait for Rimediotti to read the paper. I didn't understand a fucking word of that article!"

"Oh, weren't you supposed to be Einstein? My brain weighs so much, my brain gives me arthritis from how much it weighs . . . Enough with your brain."

"Grandpa," Massimo said, "a comment every now and again is amusing, one every ten seconds isn't. We end up listening to you and getting distracted from what you're reading."

By now, Massimo was resigned to the idea that the old-timers would continue to discuss the murder. All right. But at least let me understand the article, he thought, with everything I have to do I'm damned if I'm going to find time to read it myself. Rimediotti's already irritating enough, it's as if he's reading in block capitals, and he spells every word he doesn't know.

"You're right, Massimo," Aldo said. "You sound like the footnotes in an old book. Read what's written and keep the comments for later."

Muttering something about young and old all being Fascists, Grandpa Ampelio went back to the paper and finished the article without further comments. It didn't say much more, apart from the fact that "the police have not revealed anything" about the motive P.G. might have had for killing the girl.

"In other words, they don't know a fucking thing," was Ampelio's gloss on that, and this time nobody objected, except for Del Tacca, who asked polemically, "Oh, and you do?"

"No, I don't know anything."

"But there really are too many things that point to him," Aldo said. "He's tall, nobody knows where he was that night, and is it a coincidence that the murderer waited until the disco closed to hide the body? Come on!"

"I'll admit that," Del Tacca said. "But I need more. Why would he have killed her, in your opinion?"

"Because he'd knocked her up!" Ampelio exploded. "Maybe she didn't want an abortion, and he killed her."

"Yes, and then Savonarola came along and gave him a medal!" Del Tacca said. "Come on, Ampelio, we're not living in the Middle Ages anymore."

"Well, I think it's possible," Aldo said. "Not in cold blood, maybe not. But how often do you hear about guys who kill girls who've dumped them, or things like that? When you were young, if a girl had suddenly come out and told you you'd knocked her up wouldn't you have panicked? So then you take someone like P.G., with the kind of life he leads . . . "

"I don't know," Rimediotti, who had come in a minute earlier and stood aside to enjoy the discussion, now piped up. "In my opinion, even if he knocked her up, there was no need to kill her. What do you think, Tiziana?"

Tiziana, who was in the middle of cutting the rolls and didn't stop, replied acidly, "I think 'got her pregnant' is a perfectly good term that everyone understands immediately, and if anyone uses an expression like 'knocked her up' again, I'll poison his amaro."

"Narrow minded . . . " Ampelio muttered.

"Well, say what you like," Del Tacca resumed, "but in my opinion, the police don't have a motive of any kind."

"You're absolutely right," said the doctor, who had just come in. "Not even the one you're talking about."

Ta-dah! The effect is magnetic. Enter the doctor and everyone turns, as if Claudia Schiffer had just walked in.

"Hello to the pathology department," Massimo said. "Are you having a drink?"

"If I'm allowed to decide, yes." For some reason, the doctor's tone was slightly sharp.

"Of course you can decide. What a question! You can order whatever you like." Massimo sounded like a documentary on professionalism. "Whether you get it in what you'd consider a reasonable time is another matter entirely."

"All right. But bear in mind that my mouth's dry, and it isn't easy to talk when your mouth's dry. And that's a pity, because I have a lot of things to say. A cappuccino, please."

In silence, Massimo went to the machine and started preparing the foam.

"Dammit, I'd like to try that too," Ampelio said.

"I don't think so," Massimo replied in a neutral voice as he placed the cup on the saucer. "For once, I'm curious to hear what you have to say."

The silence was heavy with curiosity. For a few moments, at least. Something along the lines of: We all want to ask the same question. Who's going to ask first, though? Is anyone going to make up his mind? Why are we all so polite suddenly?

It was Aldo who assumed the responsibility. "All right," he said in a soft but resolute voice. "What's the story with the motive?"

The doctor sipped at his cappuccino triumphantly. Then he put his cup down on the saucer and sat down on one of the stools at the counter.

"Ah, yes, the motive. I'm only telling you this because you'll find out tomorrow anyway. The lab was besieged by reporters. Can you imagine those dumb specialists missing an opportunity to blurt it all out?"

He paused for effect, took a questioning and satisfied sip of his cappuccino, elegantly wiped his mouth, and crossed his legs, as if to say: Now we can talk.

"The girl was pregnant, that you already knew. And you also knew who the baby's father was, didn't you? Piergiorgio Neri, right?"

Another artful pause, and one finger held up in a negative gesture.

"Wrong. The fetus and Neri aren't even distantly related. Plus you also have at your disposal the DNA of the other suspect, who might still be involved, you try it . . . "

Incredulous looks from the members of the senate, who had understood immediately.

" . . . and bingo! A perfect match, so perfect you'd think they were fake. They're identical, that's all you can say."

Consternation.

"Bruno Messa?" Aldo said.

The doctor nodded gravely and finished his well-deserved cappuccino. "Precisely. And that makes things more complicated. Obviously, it's much harder now to link Alina and P.G. It also seems that this other fellow didn't tell the police everything he knew. It's natural to be distracted when you're making a statement, but some things you really should remember. Anyway, it wasn't so much that I was expecting the question of the baby to be decisive, but dammit, if they had asked me to bet on who the father was . . . "

"Why, were you so sure of winning?"

The tone, the tone. It's always the tone you ask a question in that matters. The same question, asked in two different tones, can lead to an answer or a fight. In this case, the tone of Ampelio's question didn't indicate any genuine curiosity about what the doctor believed, it was more of heavy-handed reference to the victim's virtue, especially in the "chastity and moderation" department. Which was why it was only the doctor's politeness and the inappropriateness of hitting an octogenarian over the head with your chair that avoided a barroom brawl like something out of a Western.

Inevitably, though, the conversation stopped for a moment. One moment was enough for Tiziana to enter the discussion for the first time and ask, "So what now?"

Whether out of provocation or admiration, the doctor replied directly to Tiziana instead of to the chorus as he usually did.

"Now we're in the shit. There are two suspects. The first one definitely can't have committed the crime, and so he's released. The second one, who by the way is the culprit"— exaggerated nods from the old men, who were again trying to pose as a select audience—"spent a night that seems cut out expressly to incriminate him, but since we're in Italy and not among the Taliban, or in the United States, you can't condemn someone without evidence. And in this case there isn't a single shred of evidence. Not one. Moral: in a few months they'll release him and he'll be interviewed by the gossip magazines, sitting at a café table with some gorgeous but oh-so-understanding bimbo, sipping a Daiquiri and talking about how much he suffered in prison and how his life was devastated by the experience."

*

The doctor turned, and drew the threads of his arguments together for the benefit of the pensioners.

"It's all over, you'll see. It isn't possible to establish a definite connection between Alina and P.G., not with all the thousands of people gravitating around them, who'll give seventy different versions between them. He'll be released with profuse apologies, they'll spend a few more months pretending to investigate and then file him away in the History drawer. Then one day, we'll be watching television and we'll catch a late night show where they talk about the Costa murder, reconstruct the events, and interview the people involved. And that's when we'll finally realize that it's over, that Alina's dead and we can't do anything about it, not even play detective because we'll have lost the urge."

"I haven't lost the urge yet." Massimo's voice, coming from behind the counter, was calm. No declarations, just an observation. "Forgetting about babies, what reason could P.G. have had to kill Alina?"

"I don't know, Massimo. I don't know."

"Neither do I. But that doesn't mean I can't find out. You know, whenever they asked Newton how he could solve such complicated problems, he'd reply that it was easy, you just had to keep thinking about them. I'm no Newton, that's for sure . . . "—a pause to pour himself some tea—"but if I don't understand something there's no way to get rid of it, I worry about it all day every day until I understand it."

"And if you don't?"

"Oh, no need to worry. Sooner or later I think of a new problem and forget all about the old one."

ELEVEN

"No, it's pointless. I give up. I don't understand a fucking thing."

Comfortably seated at the wheel, with the seat, his white shirt and his back nicely stuck together by a full quart of sweat in spite of the open windows—the air conditioning having broken down a month earlier—Massimo was traveling along the highway toward Rosignano. He was going to the sea, the real sea, in the Maremma, not like in Pineta where the water's so murky you can't see your feet even when it's less than half an inch high, and nothing was going to make him lose his good mood. Plus, when he was in his car, he could talk to himself as much as he wanted and nobody gave him a dirty look—they probably just thought he was talking hands free on his cell phone.

Massimo often thought about how a car changed your personality radically. More specifically, he thought about it every time he flew off the handle at other motorists whose crime was to occupy the same road that was his by right even though they couldn't drive to save their lives. If the same people had cut in line while he was waiting his turn at the bakery, they would have gotten a shake of the head from him at most. But when you're in a car, you're in your shell, alone with yourself, so you can be completely honest and you aren't scared of possible social consequences, like nasty looks or punches. You can afford to lose your temper. The other people aren't people, they're actors on a mobile TV screen, strange goldfish that pass you by, some too fast to make out, others too slow to be allowed to drive legally, like that old man in the hat just in front of me, forty miles an hour on the highway, but you'll see, the day they make me transport minister, there's no way anyone over seventy will be allowed to drive.

"Anyway, let's recap. The stupid kid can't have killed anybody, at least not at the time she died, and that's a fact. He had time to make her pregnant, though, and that's also a fact. Whoever left the body in the trash can by the pine wood, if it's someone different than the murderer, is more than six feet tall. Fact. And that asshole overtaking me on my right is another fact. AC 002 NY. I hope you crash."

Outside, the hills flowed by gently like waves of grass and earth, and Massimo sometimes distracted himself by looking at the landscape.

He switched on the car radio, just in time to catch the beginning of a song he liked a lot—*Walk Like an Egyptian* by the Bangles—and didn't think about anything while the song lasted. Then, when the music gave way to some crazy idiot with an overly friendly manner, he switched off the radio and started talking to himself again.

"Hypothesis. P.G. has some other motive we don't know about. Maybe he found out the girl was pregnant and thought it was his. But do you kill someone for that? I certainly hope not. I mean, you can't, not really. But then, why would a guy like P.G. kill someone? Why do people usually commit murder? Well, if we were in a book by Agatha Christie you'd kill for money, or because you thought your first wife was dead and so you remarried and then your first wife shows up and you have to get yourself out of the mess, so you shut her up in a room with a crocodile and it's all settled. In the Nero Wolfe books, on the other hand, it's always blackmailers being killed by their victims, fathers preventing their daughters from marrying, and so on. You always kill on the rebound, to obtain something. You don't kill someone because you hate him, you remove an obstacle. That's in books. But in real life, you almost always kill your mother-in-law because she's been breaking your balls for the past twenty years. So why would a real-life P.G. kill? Jealousy, no. I don't think he gives a fuck. Blackmail, maybe. But what could he have been blackmailed about that made him scared enough to kill? Drugs, maybe. You work in a big disco, you see lots of people. It's possible. In fact, it's quite likely. The girl probably knew something about the drugs, seeing that she went out with Messa who'd even sniff Totti's socks if they were chopped up fine enough. What the hell, I could care less. It's up to Fusco now, let him deal with it. I have to stop thinking about it or I'll go crazy. Right now I'll stop at a diner, have a good crap, and then keep going."

Having spotted a diner, he switched on his indicator and was about to move into the lane when a black Porsche overtook him and slipped in front of him, blocking his way. Cursing, Massimo braked with a screech of tires.

When he entered the diner, his legs were still shaking.

Massimo was on his way back, tired and happy and with his skin puckered by the saltwater, an unpleasant memory of a pleasant bathe, when he started to think again about the murder. Compared with the morning, when his thoughts had been tangled and incoherent, now, late in the afternoon, each idea came to him slowly, let itself be examined from every angle, and joined his other ideas in the order that seemed right. The drug hypothesis, for example, made perfect sense. But if he had to be pernickety (and he had always been good at that), there was something else that made less and less sense. It was something the lawyer had said at dinner the previous night, and that kept coming back into his head. Which was that the girl had been killed around midnight. Yet, strangely, nobody had seen her in the hours preceding the crime, either at home for dinner—hardly surprising since she had actually phoned her mother to tell her she was going out to dinner—or after dinner. She hadn't gone anywhere where anyone knew her. Either she had been out of the house on her own for three or four hours, or else she had already been with her killer. In that case, P.G. came back into the picture. He hadn't gone to dinner at the Boccaccio as he usually did, and he'd gotten to the club late. Then everything started to make too much sense. There was too much overlap between the hours when there was no trace of P.G. and those in which nobody had seen Alina.

Listen, he told himself, let's go back to the bar, then we'll see. If anything new happens, you can bet the old folks' home will know it before anyone else.

Back at the bar, he was surprised to see Del Tacca and Grandpa Ampelio still sitting outside, while both inside and outside the usual groups of idle young people were starting to gather for the aperitif, something to keep them going until their unearned evening ration of food. At the same time, the doctor get down off his usual stool at the counter, came out, and greeted him by touching an imaginary hat.

"Where are you going for dinner?"

"Tonight, home. My wife doesn't want to go out. I may go out myself later. See you tomorrow."

Yes, see you tomorrow. Before the murder, the doctor, like so many others, had been in the habit of dropping by the bar once a week. Now he seemed to find an excuse to come in every day for an aperitif or a coffee, and he'd always sit on the same stool, from whose summit, Massimo was sure, he could most easily admire Tiziana's breasts, and then he'd be off home or to his clinic.

Massimo took a chair, turned it back to front, and sat down at the table with the class of '29.

"Hello, everyone. What are you still doing here?" he asked, knowing the answer.

"Hello, Massimo," Del Tacca said. "Just chatting a bit. Rimediotti and Aldo are on their way."

"Good, I was missing you all. No dinner?"

"No, the women have all gone to the priest's charity do, but I can only stand Don Graziano when he's asleep. If he can get to sleep, of course, with all he has on his conscience, the pig. We'll be eating something here soon."

"If you bring it with you. I don't think there's much left over from the aperitif, and I've finished the flatbread."

"I'd be happy with a little ice cream," Ampelio said, casually eyeing a group of young sylphs who were gliding with ostentatious indifference along the sidewalk, displaying their marmoreal asses beneath their summer dresses.

How beautiful they are, these beauties coming back from the sea.

Weary from a long day in the sun, but still walking with the rhythm of Norse goddesses who are above the common herd. An aura of natural untouchability that confers on them an almost otherworldly appearance, a warning not to try to guess what dreams are hidden behind their dark glasses and beneath those summer dresses that both cling to their hips and flutter in the breeze. Goddesses from a remote Valhalla that may reveal itself to be some wretched nearby locality as soon as they open their mouths. Don't speak, girls, just let yourselves be looked at.

"Poor you, you'll have to do without. How many have you had today?"

"Do me a favor! With your mother breaking my balls every day about eating and cigarettes, and your grandmother always telling me not to eat ice cream and then making fried food for lunch and dinner! She'd even fry the pasta if she could! For forty-eight years I've been eating that crap, and they still break my balls about ice cream. Just one, that's all I had."

It didn't happen often, but in this case Grandpa Ampelio was absolutely right. Grandma Tilde had always cooked everything on the basis of a single, immovable parameter: it hasn't been fried enough yet.

Massimo looked at his grandfather with a touch of affection. "What kind of ice cream would you like?"

"Chocolate and yoghurt. Thanks, son."

Having gone back in the bar, Massimo called Tiziana over. "Hi. How are things?"

"Fine. How about you, did you enjoy yourself? How was the sea?"

"Perfect. Not many people about today. I found a place just past Rimigliano that's fantastic. Nobody goes there. I'll take you there one day if you're good."

"Yes, bwana. What would you like me to wear?"

"A burqa would be fine."

"When are you going to find yourself a girl, instead of playing the fool with your employees?"

"As long as I have such well-endowed employees, don't even think about it. In fact, I'm planning to introduce the *droit du seigneur*."

Massimo searched in his money pouch and took out a pack of cigarettes, a lighter, some keys, and a strange gray object, which he put down on the counter together with the rest.

"What's that?" Tiziana said. "A highway toll pass? Why did you remove it from your car?"

"I didn't remove it from my car."

"Where did you get it, then?"

"I took it from a black Porsche that had treated me like a poor relation on the highway. When I spotted it again with the window down outside the diner, I recognized it and reckoned it'd do a guy like that a lot of good to pay the highway toll all the way from Tripoli."

"You're crazy, you know."

"Listen, employee, I have to stay in here for a while. Go outside and arrange the tables, and when you've finished putting up the shot glasses make my grandfather an ice cream."

"Another one?"

"It's all right, he's not having dinner tonight . . . Hold on, how many has he had today?"

"Since I got here, four."

Massimo didn't say anything and went behind the counter. He took a knife and started slicing the lemons with extreme slowness and precision, a clear and unmistakable sign that he was becoming increasingly irritable.

Tiziana waited a few moments, then took the scoop and said, "So, how does your grandfather want his ice-cream?"

"Lemon and coffee. With lots of cream."

"Do you have an ace?"

"Three points is what I have."

"We're at the end of the game, nothing's come out yet, and you don't have an ace? You should be ashamed of yourself."

"I don't have a clue who you're with."

"I'm with you. First I gave you two, and you have eight from him, after he called the three of clubs, so do you think I'm dumb or something, to give you eight?"

"Grandpa, listen to me, give them to him. With the ace that makes fourteen, there's only one point missing. It'd be stupid."

"And what if I don't have the ace?"

"Give him three points, it'll come to six."

"Okay, here's three. What are you putting down?"

"I don't know, I'll have to put down this three of clubs, I hate to waste it for six points but if I don't get out now I'm at risk."

"You're a son of a bitch!"

"You should know, Ampelio, she's your daughter."

"Now don't you start. Play properly! If things carry on like this, I'll lose my shirt."

"But not your shoes, right?"

"What are you talking about?"

"I'm saying you came out in your slippers again tonight."

"Oh, my God, it's true. I was sure I—Massimo, are you all right?"

A justified question. Massimo had closed his eyes and had started rocking back and forth on his chair and moaning.

Ampelio waited a few seconds, then asked again, "Are you all right, son?"

Continuing to moan and rock, Massimo nodded.

"Then what the fuck are you doing?" Del Tacca asked, without an ounce of grandfatherly love.

Still continuing to moan and rock, Massimo made a sign that meant 'later' with his index finger.

He heard Rimediotti ask how long the prayer to Mecca lasted, and Ampelio answer Ihaventaclue.

After a while, Massimo opened his eyes, said "Good," got up and went inside the bar.

Four pairs of eyes followed him closely, if irritably, from behind presbyopic glasses.

He sat down on a stool, asked Tiziana something, took out all the things he had in his pockets, put them on the counter, and leaned forward. He looked at them with an affectionate smile, then picked them up one by one, and put them back in his pockets.

He came out a second later, still smiling, with his car keys in his hand.

"What are you doing?" Aldo asked, half amused, half astonished.

"I'm going to find someone."

"What about the game?"

"We'll finish when I get back."

"And what do you have to tell this person that's so important?"

"That I know who killed her daughter, and I also think I can prove it. I just need a bit of information."

Calm down, just calm down, or you're going to make a fool of yourself. I feel like the main character in that book by Sciascia, *A Simple Story*, when his superior tells him where the light switch is in the room and he understands the whole thing, who the murderer is and how he did it. And like him, I don't know who the fuck to tell. Alina's mother, yes, strange how in my head "that girl" has become Alina. A name read in the newspapers and a waxen face sticking out of a trash can have become a person. A real person, of course. Someone who lived, drank, loved, and put her trust in the wrong person. I don't feel at ease now. As long as it was a game, an exercise, it was fine. But now . . . look, it's not your fault. This thing landed in your lap without your looking for it, and now that you've understood what happened you just have to prove it. It's not that you think it's a good explanation, it's simply the right explanation. Period. Even if it's unpleasant. You can't do anything about that. Maybe it's best if I start by going to see Fusco. First, though, a shower and change. The only time in my life I discover a murderer, dammit, I really can't do it with salt on my skin, wearing a Daffy Duck T-shirt.

". . . 'confessed that he was the person who murdered Alina Costa and carried the body to the place where it was discovered, in the parking lot by the Belvedere pine wood. The accused man's defense attorney has asked for a psychiatric report on his client, insisting that he could not have been of sound mind at the time of the murder.' Oh, very convenient. That's how they all get out of it, not being of sound mind. Does that mean if I go to the town hall and tell them I was drunk when I got married, I can then go to my wife and tell her to get the hell out of my life? I'd like that."

"Calm down, Ampelio, they're not going to say he wasn't of sound mind."

"That's the least they can do! That son of a bitch . . . Just as the least they can do, it seems to me, is give the boy a medal, because if it wasn't for him . . . "

The boy, in other words Massimo, was leaning on the counter, calmly eating a croissant. It was the beginning of September, and the season was practically over. These days, the people who came in during the morning were almost all local, and they didn't want a coffee, but a story, which was why it was pointless pretending to be just a barman. So there he was, surrounded by the old-timers gazing at him as if they themselves had made that fine head capable of solving a nasty case like this, as well as various other customers all hanging on his every word.

"While we're about it," Ampelio said with ill-concealed

pride for the third or fourth time that day, "you might as well tell them all what you did."

At which Massimo, proudly but obediently, started all over again from the beginning, for the benefit of those who hadn't been there before. He recounted how O.K. had told him when, more or less, the poor girl's body must have been put in the trash can, how he had noted that the killer must have been tall, and how he had come to suspect P.G.

"The alibi poor P.G. gave the police turned out to be true. The young guy at the San Piero pharmacy, who's a friend of his, told me he had sold him a box of Imodium at about half past midnight. Except that it seemed such a joke, nobody believed him at first."

And that was how, between one visit to Fusco and the next, he had reached the moment of release. Emotional release, that is, not the release of P.G., although that had happened too.

"When Pilade pointed out that grandpa had left home in slippers, I recalled that Alina was also wearing slippers when she was found. Not flip-flops or fur slippers, like they wrote in the paper, but a pair of white orthopedic overshoes, the kind doctors wear in hospital. Not something you put on to go out. So I started to think that she must have been at home when she was killed. But that's not possible, I told myself, because she was killed between eleven and one, and at that hour she couldn't have been at home, because . . . anyway, I was distracted for a moment and I looked around a bit . . . and suddenly I saw the stool at the counter."

Pause for effect, a cigarette somehow lighting itself, I must have smoked forty since this morning, but what the hell. That was the crucial moment, the moment he had really felt like Poirot suddenly understanding everything. With a clear head, without racking his brains, he had noticed something he'd had right in front of his eyes for ages.

Dr. Carli was also very tall.

*

"In the whole of this business there were some things that didn't make sense, starting from when I first became involved. I go to a parking lot at five in the morning, convinced I'll have to explain to a drunken high school student the difference between an inflatable doll and a flesh and blood woman, and I find myself looking at a trash can with a girl's head sticking out of it. I didn't see the reflection of a boot buckle, or anything like that. No, I saw her face staring right at me. Whoever had put her in there either hadn't wanted to waste time hiding her properly or had deliberately left her like that. I was a little skeptical that someone would risk hiding a body in a trash can and then leave it just any old how. On the other hand, if it had been put in full view on purpose that meant that whoever had left her there wanted the body to be found as soon as possible. Does that make sense?"

All the heads nodded.

"So, if we start with the fact that the murderer left the body that way intentionally, we reach the conclusion that he wanted the body to be discovered as soon as possible. And that's where I find the first thing that doesn't make sense, which is that neither P.G. nor Messa have an alibi for the night. To be precise, Messa had one but would have preferred to avoid using it. That doesn't fit very well with the murderer's eagerness to have his crime discovered as soon as possible, a crime committed in the very period when it wasn't possible, or desirable, to reconstruct their movements, that is, between eleven and one. Secondly, we have two possible suspects. One of the two doesn't have either an alibi or a plausible motive. The other may have had a motive, but definitely has an alibi for the period when the murder took place. One doesn't have a motive, the other doesn't have the opportunity. In a nutshell, it doesn't make sense. Do any of you know what an axiom is?"

The senate remained silent.

"I thought as much. An axiom is a proposition that's assumed to be true because it's considered self-evident, and which provides the point of departure for the construction of a mathematical system. Every mathematical or logical system is based on axioms whose validity can't be demonstrated. Among other things, it isn't feasible to thoroughly investigate the validity or cohesion of these axioms, as Kurt Gödel demonstrated in the 1930s. In practice, Gödel demonstrated that in very coherent mathematical system, in other words every system that doesn't contain contradictions, there are true statements that cannot be demonstrated by means of the system itself. When a system investigates itself, it must accept the fact that there are truths that cannot be demonstrated."

Massimo took a deep drag on his cigarette.

"Every time I construct a system, I have to take for granted certain statements that can't in any way be proved. That's not only the case in mathematics. In real life too, we often base ourselves, whether consciously or not, on certain axioms that we don't even think of checking to see if they're true. For example one of these axioms might be that the TV news, or the parish priest, or the Party always tells the truth. Some of you may remember the old joke about the Communists believing crocodiles could fly because the Party newspaper said so. I always thought my ex-wife told me the truth, and I was very upset when I discovered it wasn't true."

Ampelio grunted. He was probably thinking more about the crocodiles than about Massimo's ex-wife.

"So let's recap: if there's something that isn't right in the way I've reconstructed the facts, there are two possibilities. One, I made a mistake in my reasoning. Two, I haven't made a mistake but at least one of the premises I started from isn't true. In the present case, what was the premise that was leading me astray?"

Pause for effect.

"The reply now is obvious. The premise that was leading me astray was the one that said that the police, and in general everyone involved in the investigation, tell the truth. That led me to consider as a given something that was actually wrong: that is, that Alina Costa died between eleven and one."

Pause, sip of tea.

"Maybe it was the fact that I'd been thinking about doctors in hospital, I don't know. I saw the stool, where Dr. Carli had just been sitting, and I thought: Of course, Dr. Carli is also tall. Very tall, over six feet. Now, I can't put what I thought in exactly the right chronological order, but remember that I'd been playing a game of *briscola* for five, and had just finished telling a pack of lies to convince grandpa that I was playing with him, even though it wasn't true. In other words, I was feeling pleased with myself for leading him up the garden path with all my bullshit. Anyway, it occurred to me that Dr. Carli is tall. And that was the starting point for everything."

Pause, a drag on his cigarette.

"So, for no reason, a few other things occurred to me. The first thing that occurred to me was that he was the person who had determined the time of the girl's death as being between eleven and one—as luck would have it, a period of time for which he had an alibi—and there was nothing else to tell us it was true. It occurred to me that anyone could send a text pretending it was from Alina if he had his cell phone on, all he needed was opposable thumbs. It occurred to me that the 'boyfriend' Alina had been having a steady relationship with, the 'boyfriend' she wouldn't even tell her best friend about, was a boy only in our heads, and that we'd never even considered the possibility that he might be a man in his fifties. And it occurred to me that the doctor had played a game of *briscola* with all of us, lying about the time of death, and that he'd also played a game with Bruno Messa, sending him a message pretending to be Alina, asking him out for dinner."

"Right," Aldo said, as if to say carry on, we're all ears.

"The reason that trick was so effective was that Alina had phoned a friend earlier to say she was going out with her secret friend. And of course the reason she kept it secret, as you all know now, was that it wasn't exactly easy for her to say she was sleeping with a man of fifty, especially a friend of the family."

Massimo extinguished his cigarette and poured himself another glass of iced tea. He looked for a moment at the glass, which was misting up with the cold, then took a particularly satisfied sip.

"Anyway, as you know, I reconstructed the evening in the following way: Alina goes to the doctor's house. He's alone because his wife's at the spa. She spends the end of the afternoon there, she even puts on a pair of slippers belonging to the doctor's wife, probably because she had just come out of the shower. She calls her friend, then . . . then what happens happens. It's about eight: the doctor sends a text to Bruno Messa, supposedly from Alina, inviting him to dinner. Then he gets dressed, takes Alina's body, and loads it in the trunk of the girl's car. Later, in the same car, which is the same color as his, the doctor goes to the Calvellis' party. That way, he gives himself a cast-iron alibi: about a hundred people see him in a very specific place and for quite a long period of time. It's highly unlikely that anyone will notice he isn't in his own car, and he doesn't want anyone coming along after he's hidden the body and taking down his license number anywhere near the parking lot. In any case, the doctor is well known among his wife's idle friends as a bit of a character, and nobody will find it strange that he came to the party in a wretched Clio, instead of his Jaguar. Couldn't he have put her in the trunk later? I don't know, maybe he was afraid that someone might come back and see him, maybe the housekeeper, whereas about nine he was definitely on his own, his son was out, and the garden of the house is quite leafy, it's impossible to look inside. So, after four, when he leaves the party, he goes straight to the parking lot, puts the girl in the trash can, then leaves the car there, the reason being that it's gotten stuck and he can't move it. I don't know if he'd planned to leave it somewhere else later. Anyway, from a technical point of view it's a perfect murder. The next day he'll say that the girl died four hours later than she actually did, and the police will take the hint. The doctor doesn't even appear on the list of suspects."

"So why . . . " Pilade said, sprawling on his chair with his belly bulging and his pants up to his sternum, butting into the speech at just the right moment, like a consummate actor, to give the narrator the right support. "What did he expect from a girl like her?"

Massimo opened his arms wide. "What can I tell you? I think Dr. Carli was really in love with Alina, and had even planned to tell his wife everything. To start a new life. Then you find that the person you wanted to start that new life with is pregnant. She tells you calmly, and maybe she even tells you the child is yours. Of course. Except that you had a vasectomy a few years ago, and being a doctor apart from anything else, you know that means there's no way you can have children. *Ergo*, from one moment to the next, you know she's been cheating on you in a big way, and the girl you've thought of as a perfect prospect for a wife is transformed into a snake woman, or a pig woman, or a combination thereof. Not only has she cheated on you, she's cheated on you with someone you consider a pimple on the asshole of the world, or someone else of the same kind. Both to be eliminated. Her physically and him legally. He must have thought that text was a stroke of genius, and in fact it wasn't a bad idea. He put the police on the wrong track for a few days, even though it wouldn't have held up. Sooner or later, Bruno Messa would have talked, it's always better to confess to daddy that you snort coke than that you strangle girls. When the matter of the murderer's height emerged, that was another big stroke of luck for him, and I was the one to give it to him. P.G., who was tall and definitely suspicious and had an alibi that literally scared the shit out of him, seemed a perfect fit. If I think about it now, I could kick myself."

"Well, nobody can say you haven't made up for it," Aldo said. "The thing that really struck me was the way you managed to find the evidence. Without that, there's no way we'd be talking here now. Fusco wouldn't even have listened to you. In fact, he'd probably have accused you of being P.G.'s accomplice and put you in jail along with his friend the pharmacist."

Massimo nodded, and started on another croissant.

He thought again about his visit to Arianna Costa, when he had told her that he knew what had happened. He had started with the evidence: the videocassette from the closed-circuit TV cameras in the garden of the Villa Calvelli-Sturani, which he'd had made from the original that very evening, a few minutes earlier, by a friend who worked in the company that handled security at the villa. He had seen again for the tenth time the images showing Doctor Carli arriving at the party in a Clio with the same license number as Alina's and skillfully parking the car, images which in their black and white banality transformed the doctor from a close friend always ready with a quip into a murderer. In a second, he had seen Arianna's face lose all the detachment and poise she had developed in her life, her eyes pitch black beneath the make-up through lack of sleep, looking at the TV set as we might look at our own house collapsing, with a question on our lips we cannot even formulate, because we already know the answer and it's too painful. Afterwards, she had walked Massimo to the door, without looking him in the face, and Massimo had been surprised not to see her cry. Probably, Massimo thought—stupidly given the circumstances—she'll cry tomorrow. Tonight she may manage to get some sleep.

To End

M any people have been crucial to this book.
I thank Serena Carlesi and Fiodor Sorrentino for persuading me to finish it and helping it to achieve its definite form.

I thank Walter Forli for his invaluable help with questions of forensic medicine and for having lent part of his name to one of the characters.

I thank Piergiorgio, Virgilio, Serena, Mimmo, Letizia, Paola, Francesco, Federico, Gherardo, Giacomo, Rino, Piero, Vittorio, Liana, my father and mother and all those who read it when it was still young and had not yet been taken up by a publisher, and told me they liked it.

I thank the Marquis and Marchioness Antinori, the Count and Countess Barbi, the Duke of Salaparuta and their other colleagues for contributing to my imagination and fluency of writing.

Last but not least, I thank Samantha, whose patience and intelligence improved the book considerably, and improved the author even more.

Pisa, August 12, 2003, near midnight